Small Farm Warriors

G S Willmott

ONWARD CHRISTIAN SOLDIERS
CHAPTER 1

A group of Australian Diggers sat beside the Albert-Bapaume Road, having marched from Albert that morning.

George Harris was the quasi-leader of the group of six friends who had survived the hell of Gallipoli, the oppressive heat of Cairo and German artillery so far. Now, they were on their way to who knows where.

'Hey George, have you got any fucking idea where we're going?' asked Sam Wilson.

'No fucking idea, mate, but I can guess it's not a luxury chateaux with a swimming pool and beautiful woman serving up ice-cold beers.'

'That's a shame. I think that'd be rather pleasant, better than the old rat- infested barn they billeted us in at Albert.'

'Isn't that the bloody truth. Speaking of Albert, wasn't that bloody church weird. The Virgin Mary leaning like that, she must have got a fucking good hit from the Krauts.'

'Yeah, don't know how she hangs on.'

'Divine intervention if you ask me, cobber, she defies the laws of gravity.'

The Leaning Virgin at Albert

The boys had about forty minutes rest, having marched for the previous three hours in full pack. It was now time to march again. Sergeant Tim Warburton was moving along the row of diggers, ordering them to get off their arses and onto their feet, ready for the next stage of the march. One digger, Mick Dwyer, protested in jest that he needed a longer break.

'Come on, Sergeant, can't we have another fifteen minutes? We're buggered.'

'No; you fucking can't. I don't know why you're complaining. you'll probably be dead in an hour or so. Get up and fall into line.'

Taking a Break

Once the five hundred men of the 1st Battalion of the 1st Division of the Australian Imperial Force were in formation, they headed off to hell, not that they were sure where this particular hell was.

The hell was the village of Pozières or rather their objective was to capture the village. They had another day's march before reaching their target. They would be footsore and weary when they arrived to fight one of the most intense and costly battles fought by the Australians on the Western Front.

George recounted his experiences in a diary.

'We came across some Tommy units returning for a rest. They waved as they marched back into Albert. I think the wave meant "go get em sucker". Quite a number of the Brits were wearing German helmets, which they had got as war trophies. We were halted on a grassy patch, with a number of other Australian units, at a place where there was a low ridge between the firing line and us. It was a pretty spot, blazing with red poppies, and sprinkled with the blue and yellow of other flowers.

There was a lot of traffic on the roads, including vehicles of all kinds, limbers, transports, handcarts, guns, and traction engines, besides horses and troops. A couple of big naval guns a few hundred yards behind us opened up once and fired a few shells back over our heads. They were fucking loud, shooting a blinding flash as they fired. There were other guns about firing occasionally also. We scored a mug of tea from a Tommy travelling kitchen nearby, God bless them.

A couple of huge 9-inch guns came along, drawn by large traction engines with caterpillar wheels. That'll put the wind up the Krauts.

At about roughly 10.30p.m. the Machine Gun Section got a move on, the other units having all proceeded towards the front. Eventually, we arrived at our destination if you could call it that… but at least we could rest for a while before the attack.

We had just got comfy when we were ordered to get up and get into formation. Apparently, we had been marching down the wrong fucking road. God help us if our officers can't even work out what road we're meant to be on.'

As they marched, Bluey Herbert started up, *Waltzing Matilda*, and soon the whole battalion joined in, singing their unofficial national anthem. Once they had all sung their favourite song half a dozen times or so Jimmy Wallis started up the derivative;

Fighting the Kaiser, fighting the Kaiser,
Who'll come a-fighting the Kaiser with me?
And we'll drink all his beer,
And eat up all his sausages,
Who'll come a fighting the Kaiser with me!

Albert Grimshaw, one of the band of six, yelled out at the top of his voice, 'German bomber nine o'clock!'

Everybody around him jumped into the drain running beside the road. Soon the message was relayed to the entire battalion and men were jumping into the drain on either side of the road. The AEG G.IV came in low and dropped bombs along their lines, killing eight diggers with the first pass. One of those killed was young Mick Dwyer. The irony!

The noise was enormous but worse was the sight of arms, legs, and heads flying through the air.

The bomber did a wide turn and headed back, dropping several bombs, following the road to the point where the first soldiers in the line were cowering in the ditch. Thirty diggers lost their lives that day, but there was much worse to come.

AEG GVI

The 1st Battalion Marching to Pozières

The Battalion had lost their motivation to sing, and they now needed to bury their dead, including all the bits and pieces strewn around the road and in the ditch.

'This is depressing, Percy, digging graves for our mates. For God's sake, we haven't even made it into battle yet!' a dejected Dick Ruby complained.

'Yeah it's the pits; poor buggers didn't stand a chance. Fucking Germans; just wait until we face them in a real bloody fight, then they'll know it! It's a lot different feeling cold steel in your belly than dropping bombs from a fucking plane.'

Once the gravedigging had been completed, the diggers were ordered into formation two abreast and continued their march in solemn silence.

After about two hours, Albert Grimshaw starting singing, *Pack up Your Troubles in Your Old Kit Bag*. Gradually, each soldier in the battalion joined in, and the stride of their steps became more purposeful.

Albert, encouraged by the response, began singing, *It's a Long Way to Tipperary*, and again the diggers joined in. These songs lifted everybody's spirits.

At dusk, they reached their rest spot for the night, the small village of La Boiselle. They secured a number of houses for billeting, and several large barns. Some of the diggers preferred to sleep under the stars instead of sharing their lodgings with a mob of hungry rats.

The usual meal of bully beef and tea was on the menu for all.

Nobody got good night's sleep; the sound of artillery in the distance and the trepidation they felt for the days ahead wasn't conducive to sleeping.

The next morning, the tired diggers woke to the familiar sounds of *Reveille*. Reluctantly, they staggered out to partake of a delicious breakfast of bully beef and tea, and once breakfast was devoured, they were called into formation for the final leg of the march to Pozières.

'Well, boys, another day of marching down this bloody road. I'll tell you what, I'm looking forward to stopping in one place for a while and killing me some Boche,' George announced.

'I'm with you, cobber. There's nothing more boring than marching for eight bloody hours, not to mention how sore my fucking feet are. I'm sure they issued me with the wrong size boots,' complained Percy Smith.

The further they marched, the louder the sound of the artillery became until the diggers couldn't hear themselves speak. They tried singing, but that was useless too. They just trudged along the road, knowing that the front was getting closer and closer.

As they neared the front line, they began passing dead soldiers lying beside the road. These were once warriors, but now they were dead bodies twisted in grotesque positions with blackened faces and hands. They had probably been there for over a week judging by how bloated they were. Their loved ones wouldn't like to see them like this. Back home, they would be referred to as "one of the fallen", a more poetic description.

At last, they reached Command Head Quarters; if a couple of dugouts could be described as HQ.

The Lieutenant commanding the 1st, 2nd and 3rd Battalions was Captain William Bannister, a solicitor back home, and regarded as a fine commander and soldier. His orders from Major General Walker were to make his troops ready for an attack within twenty-four hours. His orders in turn came from General Gough. Major Walker argued that the 1st Division had just arrived at the front having marched from Albert. His argument was based on the fact the men were exhausted and would put up a better fight if they were rested.

General Gough, known for his gung-ho approach, insisted on attacking the following night. The recipe for slaughter had begun, a recipe Gough would use throughout the war.

The attack was launched on 23 July 1916; this was to become known as the Battle of Pozières Ridge. Australian and British forces fought hard for an area that comprised a relatively high observation post over the surrounding countryside. There was also the additional benefit of offering an alternative approach to the rear of the Thiepval defences where the Germans were entrenched.

The Australian 1st Division Anzac Corps, having served in Gallipoli, was primarily given the task of capturing Pozières Ridge. This had been an objective for capture on the first day of the Somme Offensive; an objective that was never realised. The Australians succeeded in capturing the ridge by the 4th of August, having launched their offensive almost two weeks earlier. The British 48th Division assisted them in the attack.

The Australian diggers succeeded in capturing Pozières village itself, after which they moved across the main road to "Gibraltar", a German strong point. A mere two hundred yards separated the Australians from Pozières Ridge. The attack's main objective, it was heavily defended by the securely entrenched German troops. Two lines of trenches needed to be overcome before the ridge could be claimed. This action created a heavy toll on the Australian and British troops, and the Germans didn't fare much better.

Later on that first day, 23rd July, the British 17th Warwickshire Regiment joined the Australians to the north-west of Pozières village. The Germans weren't going anywhere; they defended the ridge valiantly.

The 2nd Australian Division subsequently relieved their comrades and continued the attack on the ridge for a further four days before they too were relieved. Allied casualties at this stage were running at a costly three thousand five hundred.

The ridge finally fell after almost two weeks of bitter fighting on the 4th of August. However, both Mouquet Farm and Thiepval remained under German control. General Gough insisted that his troops take these two targets and persisted with this plan, resulting in twenty-three thousand Australian casualties. Gough came under Australian criticism for his persistence in pushing the advance for five weeks. Growing scepticism of the quality of British leadership had already intensified following the notable failure of an earlier battle at Fromelles, west of Lille, on 19-20 July by the Australian 5th Division, intended to divert German attention away from the Somme.

During the Battle of Fromelles, the Australians suffered five thousand, seven hundred and eight casualties, of which a total of four thousand were fatalities; a further four hundred were captured and marched by the Germans through Lille. Their lives as prisoners of war were about to begin.

George Harris was exhausted and fed up with what seemed to be futile battles and horrendous casualties. This was not what he had signed up for, having left his mother and father and his little sister behind to try to look after the farm in the Mallee, Victoria, to fight for King and country. It didn't feel as if he was doing that, more like fighting for bloody incompetent British Generals like Gough.

General Gough

WHY DO THEY CALL IT GIBRALTAR?
CHAPTER 2

23 July 1916 Pozières

George and the band of five, Sam Wilson, Percy Smith, Dick Ruby, and Albert Grimshaw, were all waiting for the order to advance. They had been waiting for a couple of days, as Gough did not get his own way. Major General Walker ended up winning the day and the lads had a few days to recuperate from the long march.

The sound of the British artillery barrage was deafening and relentless.

'Fucking hell boys, how in the name of God could the Boche bastards survive this?'

'Fucked if I know, George, but what I do know is they'll give it back to us twice as hard when they get the opportunity.'

'Yeah, you're right there, Percy.'

'Right, cobbers, we've got to try to stick together and look out for each other. Okay?' George emphasised.

'Don't worry about us, George, we are The Invincibles of the First Brigade,' Dick said with bravado.

The barrage began to slow down, and the ANZACs were ordered to go over the top and creep towards the German lines. The idea was they would be in a good position to make a charge once the artillery ceased.

'Remember lads, on your bellies and keep your heads down,' Captain William Bannister recommended.

The Australian Diggers crawled out of their trench and began the long slow journey across no man's land on their bellies. The noise and the flares made for a firework display was nothing any of them had seen before. Dick was next to Sam, and he whispered, 'Do you hear anything mate?'

'No, it's all gone quiet.'

'You know what that means, don't you?'

'I'm afraid I do; we could be about to die.'

'Come on Sam, we're The Invincibles.'

They heard the order being passed along their line in whispered tones.

'We go at three am exactly.'

Sam looked at his watch and saw it was two fifty-five, just enough time to jot a quick note to Jessie, his sweetheart back home.

My darling Jessie,

I'm about to confront the enemy but don't worry I know I'll be fine. I'm looking forward to kissing you again my darling. Must go.

Love

Sam

Sam folded the note and placed in his top pocket. The letter would be expanded and posted after the battle.

At three am the signal was given, and the Australians began running for the German trenches. The familiar sound of German Maxim machine guns ripping through Australian flesh was heard along with the sounds of screaming and the guttural sound of men choking on their own blood.

George and Percy were able to enter the German trenches where they discovered two of the enemy waiting to greet them. George thrust his bayonet into the soldier opposing him before the German could get off a shot. Turning around, George saw Percy just standing there with a dazed look on his face.

'What's wrong with you mate? Come on we've got a job to do, there's plenty more where these bastards came from.'

Percy didn't say a word, just stood there with a vacant look in his eyes before he fell to his knees and collapsed into the trench. A bayonet thrust had mortally wounded the young soldier; at least Percy was able to kill the Kraut before dying himself.

George was horrified but couldn't stop to grieve; the warrior in him knew his duty was to keep moving through the trench shooting any Germans discovered.

Sam, Dick, Albert, and George all survived the battle to fight another day. The first battalion was successful in capturing the Pozières trench that ringed the village to the south. Mission accomplished… but at what cost?

Now there were four.

It was established by the officers that stage one of the battle had been completed successfully, and the Australians and the British had captured the German trench. Thousands had died achieving this objective.

The First and Third Anzac Battalion then moved on Pozières village itself or what was left of it. They reached the Albert-Bapaume Road. Once they had secured that location, they moved into the ruins of the village. Although pleased with their progress Command knew taking their next objective would be no picnic; the objective was named Gibraltar.

Pozières Before the Attack

Pozières After the Attack

George and his Mates at Pozières

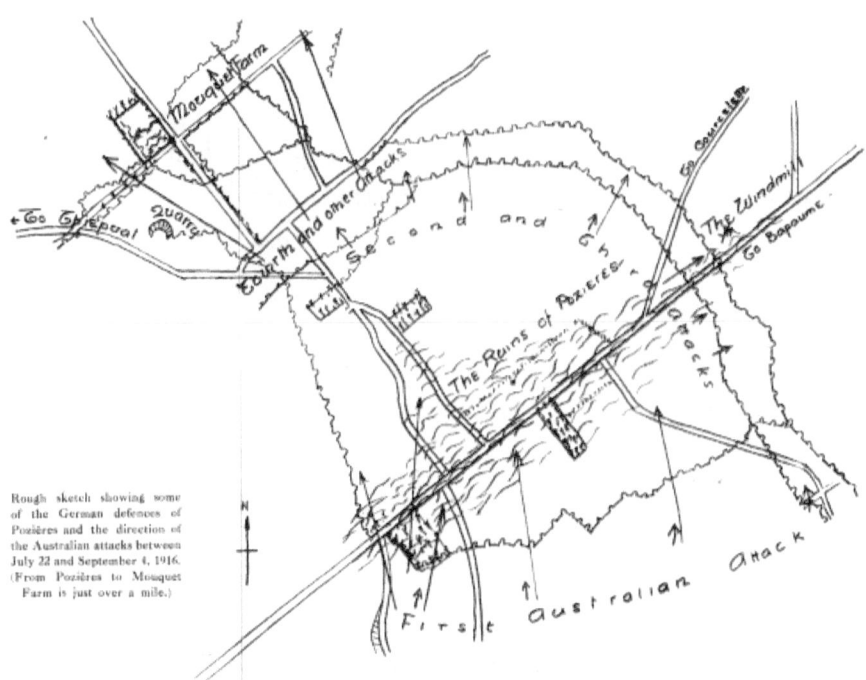

Rough sketch showing some of the German defences of Pozières and the direction of the Australian attacks between July 22 and September 4, 1916. (From Pozières to Mouquet Farm is just over a mile.)

Mud Map of Pozières

There were minimal survivors from the German garrison; those that were left retreated to the northern edge of the village. It was also intended that the old German lines would be captured as far as the road, but unfortunately the Australians failed, partly because of strong resistance from the German defenders occupying deep dugouts and machine gun nests, and partly owing to the confusion of a night attack on featureless terrain. The weeks of bombardment had reduced the ridge to a field of craters and it was virtually impossible to distinguish where a trench line had run. The failure to take the old German lines made the eastern end of Pozières vulnerable to attack, so the Australians formed a flank short of their objectives.

Two officers, Major John Jeffries and Captain Bruce Menzies, were sitting among the burned out ruins after the first day of fighting at Pozières, discussing the best way to attack Gibraltar, a large, forbidding German blockhouse on the western sector of the village. The scene surrounding them could have come from Dante's inferno; blackened trees, dead bodies strewn around and the background noise of moaning from wounded comrades. Their men had done a magnificent job in capturing Pozières against the odds. What they achieved would be the envy of the British in their disastrous campaign at the Somme.

The two officers looked up to see a British messenger running along Dead Man's Road, jumping over bodies and fallen trees, and obviously with an important message to be delivered. The messenger reached them, handed over the envelope and then slumped on the ground, exhausted.

Major Jeffries read the message, shook his head, and read it out aloud to his comrade.

'A number of cases have lately occurred of men failing to salute the army commander when passing in his car, in spite of the fact that the car carries his flag upon the bonnet. This practice must cease.'

Signed General Gough

'Where's his fucking priorities? The man's a lunatic!' complained Captain Menzies.

'I couldn't agree more. Now, getting back to Gibraltar...'

'First the bastard denies us the support we need with an artillery barrage because his reports show there are no Germans on the north side which, judging from the constant sniper fire, is bullshit. Now, just as we are about to attack the biggest ugliest German fortification for miles, the idiot tells us we have to make sure our boys salute the pompous bastard as he drives past in his Rolls fucking Royce.'

'Bruce, don't worry about him, the reality is he's completely out of touch, but unfortunately, we're obliged to follow his orders. If our diggers refuse to salute, we're obliged to give them a smack on the bottom. Now, I think we've agreed on a plan of attack, so let's go and take the bitch and kill a few Germans.'

'Yes, sir.'

The First and Third Battalions attacked Gibraltar early that day, capturing twenty-three prisoners. Their elation was short-lived; the British artillery started blasting K Trench, which was quite close to Gibraltar, necessitating the Australians' vacation of the premises.

Determined, they came back in the afternoon and captured it yet again.

The Remains of Gibraltar

Moo Cow Farm
Mouquet Farm
Chapter 3

12 August 1916

George and his remaining cobbers were in a large, reasonably dry shell hole, trying to get some sleep in the main street of what was the village of Pozières. Sleep deprivation was a soldier's second greatest enemy after the Krauts. The noise of artillery from the belligerents, the ubiquitous rats, and lice all contributed to a bad night sleep.

Reveille sounded at 4.15am. George kicked Dick who had slept through the bugle; Dick was the exception to the rule… the bugger could sleep if a shell exploded next to him.

The diggers packed their gear and got ready to move on, assembling at Pozières where the stench of dead bodies permeated the air.

George and the Boys at Pozières

They were marched about another two miles through destroyed terrain, heading for Mouquet Farm.

'Hey George, do ya think it's gunna get any easier on us from now on?' questioned Albert.

'You've got to be fucking joking, Albert; I reckon it's only gotta get worse.'

Just then Fritz got wind of the attackers and hailed them with shells. Many diggers lost their lives in the first barrage. The band of four survived yet again; maybe lady luck was playing her part.

The surviving soldiers reached their line but were told not to get too comfortable.

'Right men, we need to move forward approximately two hundred and fifty yards, and secure a new position from there. We will launch an attack on the farmhouse,' Major John Jeffries ordered. 'By the way, if you see General Gough in his Rolls Royce out there, I want you all to salute. Is that clear?'

'What the fuck is he talking about, mate?'

'Fucked if I know, but if I see Gough I'll be sure to give him the salute,' George whispered.

'I'll give you the signal to move over at 10.30pm. Is that clear? Pass it on up the line.'

The whistle was blown at 10.30pm on the dot. The Australian soldiers went over the top and ran towards their objective, Mouquet Farm.

The Germans were expecting them, so artillery fire and machine gun fire wreaked havoc among the diggers, and many died that night.

The Australians finally took possession of the farm, but at what cost? Three thousand five hundred young soldiers lost their lives in the first attack.

The four diggers were still together lying down among the rubble of what was once a beautiful farmhouse.

Mouquet Farm Before Battle

Mouquet Farm After Battle

'Albert, look what I've found.'

'Holy shit, mate, what are you going to do with him?'

'I have a good mind to shoot him in the balls but I think I'll take pity on the poor Kraut bastard,' Sam expressed with a touch of sarcasm.

'Well, we better put him to work digging our defence trench before his mad mates return,' said Albert.

The young German soldier standing in front of them looked terrified, fearing these Australians would shoot him then and there. When Albert offered him a spade the look of relief on his face was obvious. The German prisoner began digging with great gusto, ensuring that his captors would keep him at their side. The last thing he wanted to do was go back to the German front line; he'd much rather be a prisoner of war and stay alive.

Just when the boys thought they may get some shuteye, the German artillery started up again; it became a constant barrage for the remainder of the night. The casualty rate was climbing.

With the arrival of dawn, George and his mates could see what carnage had taken place overnight. There were dead bodies everywhere. Some had lost limbs, others had lost their heads… it was like a slaughter yard.

George dragged their German prisoner, assembled the other blokes and started to bury the slain as best they could. Covered, the rats couldn't get to them.

'I don't know about you blokes, but I'm fucking starving. We haven't had anything since yesterday morning,' George said.

'Yeah, I could go with a can of bully right now,' agreed Dick.

'Well, I think the bad news is we're not gunna get anything anytime soon,' George claimed.

Just then, the German artillery started up again. They could now see the enemy's position. Their shells were starting to find their mark. The diggers' appetites suddenly disappeared.

The Germans did not try to counter attack that day.

Major Jeffries ordered some men to escort the wounded and any German prisoners they had captured to the rear where the dressing stations were located. The prisoners were marched off to Albert where a POW camp had been established.

Orders came through for the 1st Battalion to move off to the left eleven hundred yards.

August 14

The rain bucketed down all night making the trenches a muddy bog; the incessant rain continued on into the day. There was a good reason why the diggers called it Mucky Farm.

'I am not happy, George. This fucking rain has drenched me down to my stinking underwear. I'm hungry, I'm thirsty and I'm in the mood to go and kill some Germans,' Dick complained.

'Well, mate, I can't help you out with the rain or your thirst and hunger, but I may be able to help you out with the killing business,' answered George.

'I suppose there's one thing going in our favour— the Boche haven't started up again with their bloody big guns.'

'No, it's been a little quiet lately. I wonder what the bastards are up to.'

Just then, their questions were answered, as shells started to fly past their heads. The Boche were at it again.

George had been recently appointed Platoon Leader and now had sixteen diggers under his command, including his remaining three mates.

George sent Dick Ruby and Sam Wilson to hold a large shell hole about fifty yards in front of the Australian line. A large shell exploded very close to where they had hunkered down. Albert was very concerned and persuaded George that he should creep over there to see whether his two cobbers were okay.

'Just keep your head down, mate, and no heroics. Tell the boys I'll relieve them in an hour or so,' George instructed.

Albert climbed over the parapet, and, keeping low, made his way to the improvised foxhole.

Albert reached the hole only to find Dick dismembered with Sam under his good mate's shattered body, shellshocked and covered in Dick's blood and brain matter.

'Sam, mate, come on… Dick's dead, but let's get you back to safety. There's a nice meal and a bath waiting for you behind the lines.'

'Fuck off! I'm not leaving Dick. He'll be all right. We need to get him back.'

'Cobber, Dick's dead. Nothing you or I can do to change that.'

'He was my best mate,' said Sam, with tears flowing down his face.

'I promise we'll bring him back, and we can bury him properly. Just for now it's too dangerous, but when the barrage has stopped you and I can come back and get him.'

'You promise?'

'I promise.'

Albert pushed Dick off Sam and helped him back to the line. The traumatised digger was taken to a dressing station where they diagnosed him with shellshock. Sam was taken back to the field hospital in Albert. He did recover and was back with his battalion four weeks later.

The Battle of Mouquet Farm - A Scenario

During the battle, the three Australian divisions of I Anzac Corps—the 1st, 2nd and 4th Divisions—advanced north-west along the Pozières ridge towards the German strongpoint of Mouquet Farm, with British divisions supporting on the left. The approach to the farm, however, was under observation from German artillery spotters who could call down barrages on the attackers from three sides of the salient that had developed in the lines. This resulted in heavy casualties among the attackers before they even reached the farm. Nevertheless, over the course of August and into September, the Australian divisions managed to reach the farm three times, only to be forced back each time.

I Anzac Corps suffered six thousand three hundred casualties and was so depleted that they had to be taken off the front for two months. As that battle dragged on, the Canadian Corps took over from the Australians who were withdrawn on the 5th of September. The Canadians captured the farm on the 16th of September, but were then pushed out by a counterattack. When the battle concluded in mid-September, the German garrison still held out in part of the farm. The farm was eventually captured on the 26th of September, following the general attack of the Battle of Thiepval Ridge by the 6th East Yorkshire Pioneers of the 11th Division who overwhelmed the last defenders with smoke grenades.

1916 - Not a Very Good Year
Chapter 4

George, his remaining mates plus the entire Division, got the grim news that they were returning to the Somme. In November they made attacks near Gueudecourt and Flers, but the wet, muddy conditions made it impossible, and they were unsuccessful. Fighting on the Somme ceased on the 18th of November, in the rain, mud, and slush of the oncoming winter.

Over the next few months, winter trench duty with its shelling and raids became almost unendurable for the diggers, though it did improve a bit when the mud froze hard.

Life in the trenches was never very easy but with the cold and snow, it became horrid.

Albert approached his Platoon Leader. 'George, I think I've got a problem.'

'You think you've got a problem? I think we've all got a fucking problem, mate what with the snow, the freezing rain, and the bloody Germans trying to kill us all. What's your particular problem, mate?'

'I think I've got trench foot.'

'Do you? Let's have a look. Take off your boots so we can see the problem.

George surveyed his mate's feet.

'For fuck's sake Albert, how long have they been like this?'

'A few weeks I suppose. Maybe a bit longer.'

'Well, mate, I'm sending you back to the dressing station. I reckon your feet are going to drop of any minute now.'

Albert was escorted back behind the line. The doctor who first examined him diagnosed trench feet with gangrene starting to develop. Albert was first sent to the field hospital then shipped to England where he was admitted into Eccleston Hospital in London.

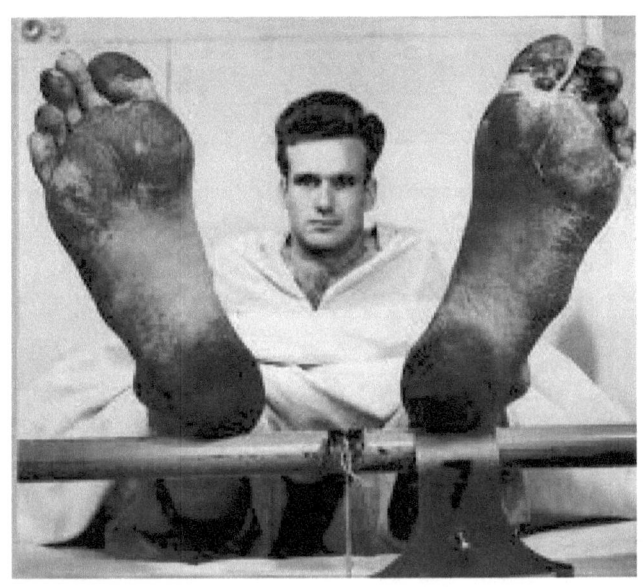

Albert remained there for six weeks and was then shipped back to his battalion in France.

While in hospital, Albert had time to write to his wife, Annie. He regarded himself as a very bad letter writer, but there was no excuse not to write now.

My Darling Annie,

I am writing to you from my hospital bed in England. Don't be alarmed, sweetheart; I'm not wounded. I picked up this thing they call trench feet. The doctors tell me I got it by stomping around in wet muddy trenches for months.

I'm making hay while the sun shines, lying back in bed between clean white sheets, and to tell you the truth, the food's not half-bad. Better than the bully beef and stale biscuits I've been eating since I got to the front.

The fighting has been pretty intense and we've lost lots of blokes from the Battalion. I really can't see how anyone can win this war; we are both in trenches facing each other and every now again we attack them and then it's their turn to attack us. There is very little territory won or relinquished.

The land looks like... actually, I don't know what it looks like. There isn't a tree alive or a bush. There are no birds or rabbits or any wildlife. The land is pockmarked with huge shell craters and in battle the smoke hangs over the landscape like a dense fog.

Anyway I'm alive and can hardly wait to see you and little Levi really soon.

As you know, I'm not much of a letter write so I'll sign off with much love.

Your Husband

Albert

'George, I think Albert's lay up in hospital in London is the way to go. A comfortable bed, pretty nurses caring for him plus heating and no Boche trying to kill him. I think I should shoot myself in the foot and join him.'

'Don't be stupid, Dick, they shoot soldiers for doing that.'

' Well maybe that's not a bad option either. Anything would be better than what we've got to put up with here.'

'I know it's hard, mate, but I'm sure things will get better when spring arrives. No more fucking snow and freezing winds to taunt us.'

'Yeah, just flies and lice and more rain.'

'I don't know what's worse, mate; sitting around in this shit hole or fighting the bloody Germans. I think I'd prefer fighting the bloody Germans. We haven't had any real action for months.'

George and the boys got their wish. the next full-scale engagement was The Third Battle of Ypres – Passchendaele. Be careful what you wish for!

October 28, 1916

By mid-1916, there were insufficient new volunteers to cover the AIF's massive casualties and to meet the British authorities' requests for reinforcements... or cannon fodder as General Haig regarded them.

The Prime Minister, Billy Hughes, appealed directly to all eligible men to volunteer. His plea was supported by the work of patriotic organisations, and a campaign of propaganda posters, to raise more volunteers.

Enlist ! Enlist !

Keep Our Wicket Up!

A well-known citizen has brought to the Committee a letter received by last mail from his son, from "Somewhere in France." This soldier said, inter alia :—

"I have just come out of the trenches after being there for three days up to my waist in cold mud all the time—no sleep. I was lucky to get out so soon, but some reinforcements happened to come along in time. I have known men twenty days in the trenches under almost similar conditions, who could not be relieved because there was no one to send to fill their places. Send us all the men you can ; it will end the war sooner, and save many persons' lives. You people in Australia don't seem to realise this ; you don't seem to realise either that **our reinforcements can only come from men you send from the Commonwealth,** for the British battalions have to be reinforced by the chaps enlisting in 'Old Blighty,' and they can't help us. It is wonderful how cheerful the boys are. So long. Send us a junk of sunshine if you have any to spare ; anyway, send more men !"

J. NEWLAND, Chairman State Recruiting Committee.

Enlist ! Enlist !

Advertiser Print, Adelaide.

2940.3c_08.1f

27

When it became apparent that the recruitment targets would not be met, the government sought approval, by way of a referendum on October 1916, to require men conscripted into militia training to also undertake overseas service. The referendum of the 28th of October 1916 asked Australians:

'Are you in favour of the Government having, in this grave emergency, the same compulsory powers over citizens in regard to requiring their military service, for the term of this war, outside the Commonwealth, as it now has in regard to military service within the Commonwealth?'

As there were 1,087,557 in favour and 1,160,033 against, the referendum failed.

'So what do you think about the referendum not getting up mate?' asked Sam.

'Well, Sam, I'm pretty happy it didn't. Here, we are up to our arses in mud and slime being shot at by people we've never met and being ordered to salute fucking Generals as they swan past in their nice clean uniforms in their toffy cars. And then there are the pricks that don't want to enlist, stay in Sydney or wherever, take our girls out and have a good old time. I don't want those pricks fighting reluctantly by my side,' answered the recently returned Albert.

'Yeah, I'm with you mate. Although I hate this war I'd much rather be here with me mates than being shipped back home as a mental case. Nearly happened.'

'Yeah, it's good to have you back, Sam.'

1917-Not Much Better
Chapter 5

After the heavy casualties at Pozières and Mouquet Farm, the First Division was withdrawn from active fighting and transported in a fleet of London buses and then transferred to trains for the remainder of the trip to Ypres.

'Well, boys, here we are in lovely downtown Ypres; not much here is there?' commented George.

'You could say that, mate. The word is, we need to get to Poperinge about ten miles away. They reckon that's where the real action is,' suggested Sam.

Located in the West Flanders region of Belgium, near to the border with France, Poperinge was located just behind Allied lines and served as an R&R spot for Allied troops. Allied soldiers knew the town as "Pops". Most of the British soldiers who fought on the Western Front passed through Poperinge. The town served as a major British supply base and garrison for the front.

Poperinge also became the hub for informal social life for Allied soldiers, particularly British and Australian troops, during the war. "Pops" provided soldiers with a brief reprieve from the harsh life of the trenches and the front. A thriving black market trade developed, with British military supplies being sold at inflated prices. The town also had numerous cafés, estaminets (bars or pubs) and brothels, which were frequented by the troops. Poperinge was a safe place for Allied troops and supply depots because it lay just beyond the range of German artillery.

The three Australian soldiers decided to head for Pops and see what mischief they could get up to.

On arrival, they hopped off the train and walked into the square, where they were amazed at the number of troops frequenting the cafés and hotels. They'd made the right decision.

Train Station Poperinge

They started up a conversation with a British Tommie in one of the pubs they had chosen for some light refreshment.

'So this is your first time to Pops, fellas?'

'Yeah, how about you?'

'Been here three times now. I reckon I know this place pretty well.'

'Any suggestions for three Aussies on first leave?'

'Well, that depends on what you're after. If it were peace and serenity, I'd recommend Talbot House. It's a top place to just relax, play some cards, drink coffee or tea and partake in some good conversation.'

One of the centres of social life for soldiers in Poperinge during the First World War was Talbot House. Reverend Philip "Tubby" Clayton and Chaplain Neville Talbot established Talbot House in 1915 as a club for Allied soldiers. Talbot House was named for Chaplain Talbot's younger brother, Lieutenant Gilbert Talbot, who had recently been killed in the vicinity of the nearby villages of Hooge and Zillebeke.

Reverend "Tubby" Clayton was a short thirty-year-old vicar in the Anglican Church. The pastor had arrived in Belgium in November 1915 and was assigned to serve as the military chaplain to the British 16th Infantry Brigade. The previous chaplain for the 16th Brigade had been killed the month before.

When Reverend Clayton visited Poperinge, he observed that aside from cafés, drinking spots, and houses of prostitution, soldiers had no places to go in the town. Clayton wanted to establish a place for soldiers to gather that was removed from the debauchery that characterised many of the other places that Allied soldiers frequented. This was the place being recommended by the Tommy.

'Sounds pleasant, but we were hoping for a bit of slap and tickle if you know what I mean,' said Sam.

'Oh, I see, then I recommend the best bawdy house in Pops "Maison de Plaisir".'

'Now, that sounds what we're looking for. How much do they charge?'

'That depends on how much time you want. Half an hour will set you back two and a half francs. It's five francs for an hour.'

'Bloody hell, it's not cheap, is it? Still, we've all got plenty of money so that should be okay.'

'Yeah, with what they pay you bastards, it shouldn't be a problem.'

'You should ask Haig for a pay rise.'

'Yeah, sure.'

The three diggers followed their newfound friend's instructions and found "Maison de Plaisir" two streets away.

George, being the leader, knocked on the brightly coloured door. A rather plump middle-aged woman let them in. Her name was Madam Fifi.

Madam Fifi

'Madam, we would like to avail ourselves of one of your girls,' explained George.

'You just want one? It can be arranged.'

'No, I am sorry… you misunderstand me, I meant a girl each.'

'Oh, of course, how long would you like?'

'I think one hour. Is that okay?'

'Of course. That will be five francs each.'

The three virgins paid their hard earned money over to Madam Fifi; the madam led them into the waiting area. The stairs leading up to the fourth storey were crammed with soldiers, mainly Australians.

'For fuck's sake, there must be half the First Division waiting a turn,' George remarked.

'Make that the whole First Division!' Sam exclaimed.

The boys waited their turn and the wait was worth it. After an hour of lovemaking, they met out in the street.

'How good was that, fellas?'

'Good enough to want to go back tomorrow night,' laughed Albert.

They all agreed and returned to "Maison de Plaisir" for the following three nights. They also visited Talbot House in the early evening for some quiet time and a game of Gin Rummy.

It was during one of these visits to Talbot House that they discovered from a notice stuck to a wall that the Australian Government was introducing a scheme for returning soldiers.

THE THIRD BATTLE OF WIPERS
CHAPTER 6

Menin Road

November 1916

The 1st Division had been informed by High Command that they would be rested in Ypres for the winter months. This suited George, Sam, and Albert, as they enjoyed their regular visits to Poperinge and all the delights the town offered. This sojourn was not as long as they had hoped for.

Flers Before Battle

Flers After Battle

The rain was heavy and persistent, and the battlefield was a wet muddy quagmire.

The British had been searching for a solution to penetrate the German trenches without sacrificing thousands of soldiers in the hope some would make it through. The casualty rates were extremely high, which was becoming very unpopular on the home front.

A new weapon was needed to break the stalemate.

In 1912, an Australian, Lance De Mole, submitted a proposal to the British War Office for a "chain-rail vehicle which could be easily steered and carry heavy loads over rough ground and trenches." Two years later, a tank, designed and named by Swinton, was adopted by the British. The design was very similar to De Mole's.

De Mole's Tank Design

Lance De Mole

In 1914, Lieutenant-Colonel Ernest Swinton, proposed the development of a new type of fighting vehicle. The armoured vehicles being used by both sides were ineffective against the enemies' trench network. Caterpillar tracked vehicles were already in France, as the British used them as heavy gun tractors, and this was the type of propulsion recommended.

Lieutenant-Colonel Ernest Swinton

Swinton had received some support from those in authority, but many in the army's General Staff were deeply suspicious. Swinton needed a prototype of the machine, which would alter warfare on the Western Front. By June 9th, 1915, an agreement was made regarding what the new weapon should be. It should:

- Have a top speed of 4 mph on flat land
- The ability to turn sharply at top speed
- The ability to climb a 5-foot parapet
- The ability to cross an eight foot gap
- A working radius of 20 miles
- A crew of ten men with two machine guns on board and one light artillery gun.

Big Willie Tank

One supporter of the prospective new weapon was Winston Churchill, who called the vehicle Land Battleship.

The tank, as Swinton named it, was being manufactured in Britain with significant resources allocated to the program.

The first battle to employ the tank was Flers-Courcelette, despite having only forty-nine tanks.

The attack was launched across a twelve-kilometre front from Rawlinson's Fourth Army salient on the 15th of September. Twelve divisions were employed, along with all the tanks the British army possessed.

General Haig, the British Commander-in-Chief, had wanted many more tanks in readiness for the full launch of the Somme Offensive on the 1st of July, but nevertheless determined to proceed with the Flers-Courcelette attack with this reduced number. This was seen as a somewhat controversial decision, as others in the War Office had argued that the tanks would be of little practical use in such small numbers. Winston Churchill, who had championed the development of the tank, complained, "my poor 'land battleships' have been let off prematurely on a petty scale."

These early tanks proved notoriously unreliable during testing and application. Weighing approximately twenty-eight tons, they could move forward only at a snail's pace; two miles per hour. They were impervious to small arms fire, and to a lesser extent machine gun fire. Inside the tank, the operators were required to wear chain–mail visors to protect them from the paint and metal chips flying around inside the tanks as the machine guns peppered them. The tank's greatest enemy was shellfire; a direct hit would completely destroy a tank, and many were lost.

Radio communication was not available until late in the war; carrier pigeons were used instead. This resulted on more than one occasion British tanks killing British soldiers.

Pigeon Being Released From a Tank

The attack, as was the norm, was preceded by an artillery bombardment designed to leave unshelled lanes open for the advance of the new mobile weapon. That was the theory.

Accordingly, on the 11th of September, the forty-nine tanks began to move slowly into position in the line. As a measure of their fundamental unreliability, seventeen tanks were unable to make it as far as the front line; they just wouldn't start. Of the twenty-two that did, a further seven failed to start when the attack began. Thus, fifteen of the forty-nine tanks rolled slowly over No Man's Land with the beginning of the attack on the 15th of September.

Despite all their problems, the launch of the tanks produced devastating effects upon German morale - at least initially. On a wider front, their effectiveness was limited, given their scarcity together with their inherent unreliability. The German High Command's initial reaction was that the tank could be defeated instead of imitated.

However, the British, together with the Canadian Corps, made initial gains of some two kilometres within the first three days, something of an achievement at the time particularly when comparing it to the earlier battles of the Somme. Led by tanks, the villages of Martinpuich, Flers, and Courcelette fell to the Allies, as did the much sought-after High Wood.

Nevertheless, a combination of poor weather and extensive German reinforcements halted the Allied advance on the 17th of September; the Allies had again suffered heavy casualties, including Raymond Asquith, the son of the British Prime Minister Herbert Asquith. The attack was called off on the 22nd of September.

The use of tanks had by no means led to any anticipated breakthrough, but they nonetheless impressed Haig, who requested that one thousand more be constructed.

Like their Australian brothers, the Canadians were regarded as being ferocious yet tactical fighters.

They were similar to the diggers in that they came from a large and in some areas hostile environment. They were resilient and inventive and most importantly, well led.

The three Canadian Canucks, Joe, Frank, and Philippe, were waiting for the signal to attack their objective of Gueudecourt. The rain was teeming down, and the trench was quickly filling up with muddy water. Joe offered his mates a cigarette but they proved impossible to light. The noise of the British guns made it difficult to communicate. They waited in silence with their own thoughts. Frank attempted to write a note to his sweetheart.

My Darling Sophie,

I am now waiting to go over the top and attack a place called Gueudecourt. It's near another village called Fler. It's a lovely name, and it probably was a pretty village once, just like Gueudecourt, but after we have blasted it with our big guns, and the Germans have hit back at us with their guns, it's become a muddy quagmire with blackened broken trees and dead soldiers and dead horses littering no man's land. Sophie, you couldn't imagine the smoke filled sky that blots out the sun on the rare occasion it shows its face. Mostly it's just pouring rain and cold.

I'm sorry I sound so down, but to be honest it is depressing.

I've heard the Government will give us farms if we want them. I'm seriously giving it some thought. May I ask for you to consider it? We could marry when I return and live the good life together. It seems like a million miles away, but this horrible war has got to end soon, surely.

All my love

Frank

The barrage ceased, and the boys knew it was time to climb over the parapet and head for the German occupied village in support of the British and on their flank.

Philippe whispered to his two comrades, 'Remember boys, we're Canucks; we've been through hell before and come out the other side and we'll do it again this time.'

'I hope you're right pal,' said Frank.

'You know I'm fucking right.'

The whistle sounded, Major Clooney led them out, his service revolver in hand clambering over the pockmarked muddy terrain.

Joe and his mates were caked in thick mud within one minute of leaving the trench. The Krauts were throwing everything at them, and Canucks were falling like flies.

A shell crater offered them some respite, but not for long, as they knew they had to keep advancing. The Canadians could see Gueudecourt's church spire in the distance.

Philippe figured they had about one thousand yards before they'd reach the village, but the artillery and machine gunfire were just too intense for them to make headway from their current position.

The two tanks that had been allocated were bogged down in the thick mud and became useless. Major Clooney ordered his remaining troops to retreat to their line where they could regroup.

Back in the wet muddy trench, the Canadians took the opportunity to boil the billy and make some tea. Stale bickies and jam accompanied the brew.

'Well, Frank, I told you we'd make it; Canucks survived the battle yet again.'

'For now, Joe, just for now… but no doubt we'll be out there again very soon.'

'We'll be right, pal. Just think of that farm back home. The Government is hanging onto your farm in British Columbia; it's waiting for you.'

'Yeah, I'm not so sure about that. It's what keeps me going, though, the thought of farming my own land and holding my Sophie in my arms again. If I didn't have those two things to look forward to I'd be dead like the other poor bastards we left out there.'

The orders were given to mount another attack on the German positions the Canadians ran bravely into the firestorm and eventually took the first German line. They were on the outskirts of Gueudecourt and could not only hear the German fire… they could see the bastards.

'One thing I've been dreading is using my bayonet for the first time. I've got no problem with shooting a Kraut, but sticking my bayonet in his belly is another thing altogether.'

'Yeah, I know what you mean, Philippe, seeing the bastard's eyes glaze over as you twist the blade.'

'Come on, guys, we're Canadian soldiers, Canucks. If we have to take the Germans on in hand to hand we'll bloody do it.'

'I suppose so, not looking forward to it, though.'

Just then they heard the order: 'Advance into the village, take it, and hold it.'

The three pals and the remainder of the 22nd Battalion slowly advanced on Gueudecourt. The German defence was fierce. Soldiers were falling with each yard of the advance. After about an hour, the first Canadians entered the village. Germans were hiding in the ruins and sniping the Canucks at every opportunity.

The Canadians used grenades to flush out the enemy.

Philippe was moving slowly through a cobbled laneway when a German soldier appeared in front of him. The German pointed his Mauser rifle at Philippe and pulled the trigger. Nothing happened; his rifle had jammed. The Canadian quickly thrust his bayonet into the German's throat, withdrew and thrust the blade into his belly. The enemy soldier dropped to his knees and rolled onto the cobblestones. Philippe didn't think twice before continuing the search of Gueudecourt's ruins for more of the enemy.

All three friends survived the battle and the Canadians hung onto the town for a further four days, despite German counterattacks and heavy artillery fire.

The final Battle of the Somme was over; the war wasn't.

Gueudecourt After the Battle

ARRAS
A NICE PLACE BUT I WOULDN'T LIKE TO LIVE THERE
CHAPTER 7

The First Battle of Bullecourt, on the 11th of April, 1917, was an Australian attack on German trenches east of the village of Bullecourt. The plan was to advance some three kilometres north, taking the village of Hendecourt, two kilometres northeast of Bullecourt. The normal tactics would be to support the ground troops by an artillery bombardment prior to the attack on the German trenches. However, at Bullecourt, the Australian 4th Division attacked without artillery support in an attempt to catch the Germans by surprise. The attack was made with the assistance of a dozen tanks. Unfortunately, most of the tanks didn't reach the German line. Undeterred, the Australian infantry advanced northwards, with Bullecourt on their left flank, and seized two lines of German trenches. Increasing German resistance halted them, having been let down a second time by the failure of their own artillery to fire on the German counterattacks. The Australians, having held the enemy trenches for several hours, were driven back to their starting line with the loss of over three thousand men. Poorly planned and hastily executed, the first battle of Bullecourt resulted in disaster.

General Gough again sacrificed Australian diggers' lives.

Three weeks after the first battle of Bullecourt, the Australian 2nd Division, together with the British 62nd Division attacking their left towards Bullecourt itself, assaulted over the same ground where the Australians had met defeat on April the 11th. This time, the Australian infantry attacked with the support of artillery.

On the first day of the battle, on the 7th of May, one Australian brigade on the right flank was able to reach the German first line, and the British obtained a foothold on the southern edge of Bullecourt. The main Australian attack was successful in capturing the same German trenches the Australian 4th Division had been ejected from on the 11th of April.

The battle continued for two weeks, with the Australians and British committing four more divisions (the Australian 1st and 5th Divisions, and the 7th and 58th British Divisions). The Germans, also reinforced, made numerous unsuccessful counterattacks. By the 17th of May, the Germans admitted defeat by ceasing attempts to recover their lost ground. A total of one hundred and fifty thousand men from both sides fought at Second Bullecourt, and tragically, eighteen thousand British and Australians, and eleven thousand Germans were killed or wounded in battle.

Arras1917

E03260

Australians Attacking Hindenburg Line

George and his two close mates were heavily involved in the battle; they were now under the command of Captain Percy Black.

The strategy was for the platoon to walk behind the tanks and, when the iron beasts had destroyed the barbed wire, to penetrate the German trenches and take the Hindenburg Line.

They waited as the tank operators attempted to start the two tanks; however; it didn't look as though they would be going anywhere soon.

Major Black yelled out to his men, 'Come on boys, bugger the tanks!' and charged full on into the wire. His men, including The Invincibles, leaped forward with him and fought their way into the German trenches. The diggers were the first soldiers to break through the Hindenburg Line. Once they got through, they looked for Major Black. George found him dead on the wire, his pistol still in his hand.

A Section of the Hindenburg Line

E03366

Australians in Captured Trench

'The best commander we have ever had,' said George.

'Certainly the bravest,' the others agreed.

The three soldiers dug a shallow grave and placed his body in it. They erected a makeshift cross and scrawled his name and date of death. Their hope was to be able to return and retrieve Percy and bury him with full honours at a later time.

Captain Percy Black

So many ANZACs had been killed in the attack that there were only a few left to defend the trenches. Once the Germans realised this, they mounted a counterattack and overwhelmed the diggers, who were forced to withdraw. The only order given was 'fight it out like Australians'.

The Australians returned with fresh troops three weeks later and again captured Jerry's trenches. The Germans mounted counterattack after counterattack for the next two weeks but finally gave up and withdrew.

Canada's Defining Moment

The Canadians regard Vimy Ridge with the same reverence as the Australians regard Gallipoli. Vimy Ridge was the high ground, it commanded views over the entire Douai Plain; therefore, the Allies wanted the Ridge to create a powerful position in Northern France.

It was critical to the Germans not to lose Vimy Ridge, for if they did, their position in the entire region would be jeopardised. The loss of Vimy Ridge would expose a vast amount of German held positions to the Allied guns. It also protected the Hindenburg Line; the last German defence.

Both sides were more than aware that the previous times they fought over the Ridge in 1914 and 1916, over one hundred and fifty thousand French and British lost their lives, as did many thousands of Germans.

The German defences were, as usual, formidable with barbed wire, machine gun nests and artillery. They also had an extensive network of tunnels, including very comfortable living quarters.

The battle plan was for the British forces to flank the ridge traversing across no man's land, while the responsibility for taking the Ridge was the Canadians'.

Every soldier and officer knew just how critical this battle was and how it would affect the outcome of the war.

An essential part of any campaign is the quality of the leadership. In this case, unlike at Fromelles and other battles, the leadership was magnificent.

The two commanders were Lt. General Sir Julian Byng and Major General Arthur Currie, who would lead a united Canadian force to take the Ridge. Many thought this was an impossible task.

Both these leaders had an enormous amount of experience and had seen the slaughter at Ypres and Verdun; they knew the old strategy of 'let's throw our soldiers at the German machine guns' was futile and insane.

They were going to conduct this battle with a new and effective methodology.

Byng

Currie

They knew the old method of throwing wave after wave of closely packed infantry at the German defence was wasteful. The soldiers had no defence against the machine guns and barbed wire. The results were horrendous casualties and very little success.

The Canadians developed a system of placing machine gun, grenade and rifle specialists within a single platoon. These platoons would strike at the enemy, not in a straight line, but in a more fluid action where German defenders had less chance of merely mowing down the attackers. This attack would find the attackers able to cover their own advances.

Instead of directing the battle from behind the lines, safe in a chateau, the Canadian officers were fighting with their men, keeping a close tab on what was happening on the battlefield. They briefed each man on their objective and each man received detailed maps. This would ensure that the Canadian troops were clear on the objectives, and if an officer were killed, they could continue knowing what needed to be done.

By the time the attack had begun, twenty-one miles of signal cable and sixty-six miles of telephone wire had been buried on the battlefront. The corps had dug eleven underground tunnel-ways to aid in the movement and protection of the troops. These underground roads were equipped with electricity, medical stations, supplies and rest stations. Portable bridges were built to assist in the movement of artillery pieces over the most difficult terrain and trenches.

Prior to Vimy Ridge, the machine gun was used by both the Germans and the Allies as a weapon of defence. The Canadians changed all that and used them as an attack weapon.

The machine gun fire became a supplement to the artillery barrage. During the attack, the lighter weight Vickers guns would be set up along with the Canadian advances, providing both cover and a true attacking power designed to keep the German troops from attempting their usual defence, and giving them the opportunity of repairing their barbed wire barriers.

The Canadian Forces established an enormous strike capability with their artillery; almost two hundred and fifty heavy guns and almost six hundred field guns were aimed at the German positions. The bombardment lasted three weeks, targeting Fritz's machine guns and artillery. On average, two thousand five hundred tons of shells blasted the German positions daily. German communications were destroyed, stopping food, ammunition, and replacement troops from getting to their lines.

Supplying the Canadian troops was a network of rail lines built to bring the huge numbers of shells into position. Special fuses were developed for shells that would cause an almost instantaneous explosion, designed to take out enemy's barbed wire. That was something the British could not do at the Battle of the Somme. During the week preceding the attack, the "week of suffering" as the Germans called it, over one million shells were fired at Vimy Ridge.

One of the faults with the British bombardment method was that the Germans hunkered down in their secure dugouts drinking tea and playing cards, and when the shelling ceased, they knew it was time to enter their trenches and starting slaughtering the enemy.

The Canadian plan called for artillery to keep a precise pace in front of the Canadian troops moving across no-man's-land. A well-rehearsed movement of man and shell, moving at a pace of about one hundred yards every three minutes, would provide a dangerous but effective cover for the Canadians. German machine guns were kept silent as gunners stayed protected within the tunnels and trenches. This method also afforded an element of surprise, as many Germans left their positions to face their attackers, only to find the Canadians already in their trench.

The essential difference between Vimy and other battles was the collection of good and detailed intelligence. Microphones were placed throughout no man's land, and aircraft and balloons were used to determine where Fritz's gun and artillery placement were located.

By having the information available, the Canadians were able to destroy eighty-five per cent of the German Batteries prior to the attack.

The Canadian Attack on Vimy Ridge

On April the 9th, 1917 at 5:28 am, the battle began. The weather was atrocious; a combination of snow and sleet, when the Canadians exploded their underground mines. Gas shells fell onto German positions and transportation routes, and the artillery began to blast the German positions. All hell broke loose.

Over eleven thousand Canadian and British guns opened up on the Ridge. The Canadians kept to their timetable and followed their detailed plans. By early afternoon, seventy per cent of their objectives were taken.

Thousands of Germans were taken prisoner, and many thousands more had been killed. However, still to be taken was the high ground position called "the Pimple". That was the responsibility of the British forces attached to the Canadians. Hill 145 was also yet to be taken.

By the morning of April the 10th, Hill 145 had been taken and by April the 12th, the Canadians had reinforced the British attacking "the Pimple" and it was taken as well.

By the end of the battle, all objectives had been met and the Canadians had established themselves as an elite fighting force. The German line had been soundly breached, and the Canadians had fended off any thoughts of a German counterattack.

Unfortunately, British High Command, through ineptness, did not organise British and French battalions to take advantage of the breach in the German lines. Apparently, they did not believe the Canadians would be successful because they were basing their predictions on their own track record. The offensives of the British and French failed in the following weeks.

Canada suffered ten thousand, five hundred casualties, including three thousand five hundred and ninety-eight killed in a battle which gained much, but whose gains were squandered by the generals back in their chateaux, well behind the front line.

HIT THE ROAD JACK
CHAPTER 8

July 1917

The band of three was sitting in a rat-infested trench waiting for the rain to ease. They had been occupying this inhospitable place for the past two weeks with very little action to relieve the boredom. Once every now and again George would hold up the periscope to spot any Germans that could be shot, but the pickings were few and far between; the bastards were keeping their heads down.

They were on the outskirts of a village called Passchendaele, which was located close to Ypres.

'Sam, what part of Tasmania are you from?' asked George.

'The Huon Valley.'

'Where's that?'

'It's right down the south end. If you keep going any further south you end up in Antarctica.'

'Sounds fucking cold to me.'

'Not really, not much colder than Victoria, I'd think.'

'Is that where you want to get a farm?'

'It's apple country. I want to get an orchard.'

'Did you grow up on an orchard?'

'No, my dad was the local cop at Huonville. He knew fuck all about apples, didn't even like them.'

'So, why the ambition to become an orchardist'?

'Cause I don't wanna become a cop and if the Government wants to give me an orchard I'm not gunna say no.'

'Sounds reasonable.'

' How about you, George? What's your plan?'

'It's a bit hard hatching a plan while I'm sitting in a muddy hole waiting for the order to "go over the top" and face Jerry's bullets and shells.'

'You've got to have plans. If you don't, how can you have a future?'

'I suppose you're right, Sam. I must admit I've been thinking of applying for a grant and giving farming a go.'

'Whereabouts, mate?'

'I don't really care. I grew up in Fitzroy in Melbourne. Dad was a butcher.'

'So you know a bit about cattle and sheep?'

'Na, not really. All I ever saw was carcases.'

'So you don't really care whether you farm cattle or wheat?'

'No, not really. I just want to work outside and build a profitable farm so I can raise a family.'

'I've never heard you talk about a sweetheart back home. Have you got one?'

'I did, but I got a letter from her about twelve months ago to say she's married some rich bastard that didn't enlist.'

'Jesus mate, that must have been devastating.'

'Yeah, I was pretty upset at the time. I don't care anymore.'

STAND BY YOUR OWN!

Albert returned from the dressing station after getting his feet checked. Having suffered from trench foot previously, he was required to receive regular check-ups.

'G'day boys, what are you up to?'

'We're just discussing what we're gunna do after this fucking war is finally over as a matter of fact,' said George.

'May I suggest getting drunk regularly and laying beautiful women?'

'That sounds pretty damn good to me, Albert, but no, we've been talking about becoming farmers or, in Sam's case, an orchardist.'

'I must admit I've been giving it some thought since we spoke with Tubby at Talbot House,' Albert said.

'What do you mean— laying beautiful women?'

'Well that too, but I mean whether I go back to Cairns and continue working for my father-in-law or whether I give the independent farming caper a go.'

'Well, I reckon if the Government is willing to give us a plot you'd be crazy not to give it a bloody good try,' said Sam.

'Yeah, I'm with you, Sam; it's got to be worth a go, the worst that can happen is we give the bloody farm back.'

'I'm gunna try to get some shuteye. My intuition tells me we could be up for a hard day tomorrow,' said George.

George's intuition proved to be correct; the next day marked the first day of the Battle of Menin Road.

Menin Road

Menin Road Leading into Ypres 1913

By July 1917, things were looking pretty bad, French mutinies were increasing and it was decided that the British Forces would need to take control of the Western Front. This provided General Haig with an opportunity to launch an offensive, which was what the gung-ho general wanted all along. His plan was to attack from Ypres in Belgium and drive the Germans from the surrounding ridges and, with luck, reach the Belgium coast.

Haig was gloating over his success at Messines in June and unleashed his attack on the 31st of July 1917. The British bombarded the German positions for ten days prior to the attack, using 3000 guns, which expended 4,250,000 shells. With that intensity, the Germans certainly knew an attack was imminent.

When the attack was launched across an 18-kilometre front, the German Fourth Army was in place to hold off the main British advance around the Menin Road, and restricted the Allies to fairly small gains to the left of the line around Pilckem Ridge. Similarly, the French were halted further north by the German Fifth Army.

Menin Road 1917

British attempts to renew the offensive over the course of the next few days were severely hampered by the onset of heavy rains, the heaviest in thirty years, which created a thick muddy swamp. Tanks found themselves immobile, stuck fast in the mud. Similarly, the infantry found their mobility severely limited.

The massive bombardment had destroyed the drainage systems, and the millions of shells fired had created a moonscape, making it difficult for the Allied forces to advance.

Finally, with the army stuck in the muddy fields, the bloody offensive came to an untidy close. Many would afterwards call this offensive, actually a series of battles, after the name of the village that had become the last objective – 'Passchendaele'.

Images of Menin Road

The 1st Division's artillery was in action from the start of the Third Battle of Ypres on 31 July 1917, but the infantry was not called upon until the second phase of the battle commenced on 20 September with the Battle of Menin Road. Attacking across 1,000-yard front, along with ten other divisions, including the Australian 2nd Division on their left, the 1st Division captured around 1,500 yard of ground, securing Glencorse Wood and gaining a foothold in Polygon Wood. The Australian divisions suffered five thousand casualties from the battle; the 1st Division alone lost two thousand seven hundred and fifty-four men, mainly from retaliatory shelling from heavy artillery after the advance was completed.

The noise and the chaos of dirt and body parts flying from artillery shells hitting their line were horrendous. George ordered his men to lie at the bottom of the muddy trench to try to avoid the carnage. A direct hit would have put paid to that plan. It was still raining heavily, and the trench was flooding; nevertheless, the soldiers remained where they were until called upon to go over the top.

The intensity of the German barrage was frightening. A cacophony of exploding shells made it impossible to communicate inside the trenches; hand signals had to suffice.

A shell exploded directly in front of George and his mates, collapsing the wall of the trench and covering all three in a blanket of soil and mud.

George managed to dig himself out with the aid of his helmet. When he looked around for Albert and Sam, all that could be seen was a hand sticking out of the still smoking earth. George began digging furiously and uncovered Albert. After ensuring his mate was alive, he then scanned the trench for Sam. At first, he saw nothing, then something caught his eye. It was a metal object, and when he dug down, he discovered a metal helmet. It was Sam's. Again digging frantically, George discovered his good mate, Sam was still breathing; just.

Two other 22nd Battalion Diggers appeared and helped George dig out his two mates. They were laid down in a clear section of the trench and after a short time seemed to recover their normal breathing pattern.

An officer appeared and demanded to know why two able-bodied men were lying down in the trench.

'Sir, they are recovering from being buried alive.'

George explained what had happened and how Sam and Albert were lucky to have survived.

'Can they get up?'

'I don't know, sir.'

'Well, get them up on their feet and see how they go.'

George and the other two soldiers helped the men to their feet. Although a bit shaky, they managed to stand unaided.

'Permission to escort them to the dressing station for a check-up, sir?'

'Permission denied, these men are obviously well enough. We're expecting a major attack from the Germans as soon as they cease this bloody barrage, and we need all the able-bodied men we've got. Carry on.'

The three mates moved down the trench to a spot that was vacant due to the death of soldiers that once occupied it.

The German barrage continued. A scream went out. 'GAS! GAS!'

George grabbed his gas mask and pulled it on, but Sam and Albert did not follow his lead.

'Quick, put on your masks!' George yelled.

'We don't have them; they must have been lost when we were buried,' said Sam.

George looked around and grabbed two masks belonging to diggers who didn't need them anymore.

'Here, whack these on.'

The Germans were now firing mustard gas shells. This meant that there would be no frontal attack as the gas did not discriminate between sides.

Remaining consistently ahead in terms of gas warfare development, Germany unveiled an enhanced form of gas weaponry against the Russians at Riga in September 1917: mustard gas (or Yperite) contained in artillery shells.

The serious blisters it caused both internally and externally, brought on several hours after exposure, distinguished mustard gas, an almost odourless chemical. Protection against mustard gas proved more difficult than against either chlorine or phosgene gas.

The use of mustard gas - sometimes referred to as Yperite - also proved to have mixed benefits. While inflicting serious injury upon the enemy, the chemical remained potent in the soil for weeks after release, making the capture of infected trenches a dangerous undertaking.

Sam, still feeling the effects of his burial, sustained burns to his hands and was evacuated to the dressing shed and later to the field hospital. George and Albert remained unscathed after the attack.

Australians wearing Respirators

After Menin Road, there was a five-day pause. The 4th and 5th Australian divisions took over from 1st and 2nd Divisions for the next phase.

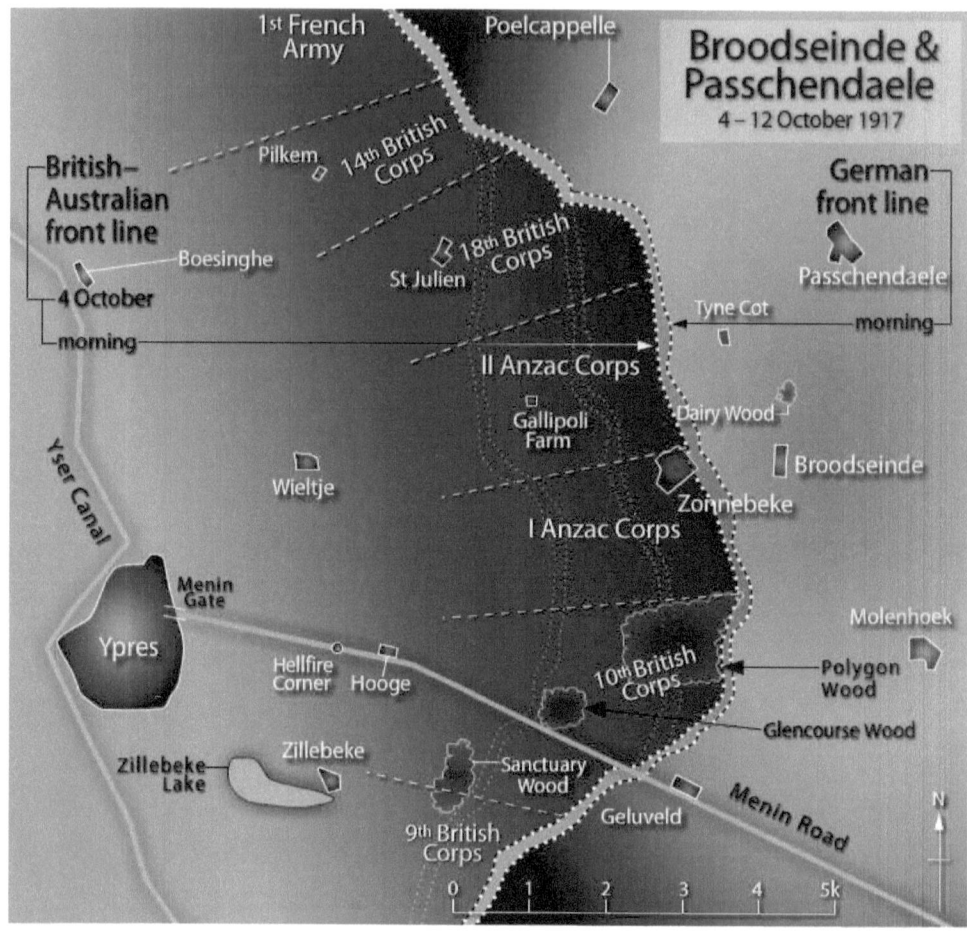

The Battle of Broodseinde

The Battle of Broodseinde was fought on 4 October 1917 near Ypres in
Flanders, at the east end of the Gheluvelt plateau, by the British Second and
Fifth armies and the German Fourth Army. The battle was the most successful
Allied attack of the Battle of Passchendaele. Using "bite-and-hold" tactics, with
objectives limited to what could be held against German counterattacks, the
British devastated the German defence, which prompted a crisis among the
German commanders and caused a severe loss of morale in the German
Fourth Army. Preparations were made by the Germans for local withdrawals,
and planning began for a greater withdrawal, which would entail the loss to the
Germans of the Belgian coast, one of the strategic aims of the British offensive.

After the period of unsettled but drier weather in September, heavy rain began again on the 4th of October, and affected the remainder of the campaign, working more to the advantage of the German defenders who were being pushed back on to far less damaged ground. The British had to move their artillery forward into the area devastated by shellfire and soaked by the return of heavy rain, restricting the routes along which guns and ammunition could be moved, which presented German artillery with easier targets.

In the next British attack on the 9th of October, after several days of rain, the German defence achieved a costly defensive success, holding the approaches to Passchendaele village, which was the tactically vital ground.

The 1st, 2nd and 3rd Australian Divisions captured Broodseinde Ridge on the 4th of October, 1917. It was a vital victory.

Then it began to rain. Five days later, the 2nd Australian Division suffered heavily in a further attack in the mud. Finally, on the 12th of October, another attack, involving the 3rd Division assisted by the 4th, was made against the village of Passchendaele atop the main ridge. In the face of heavy fire, the men fought in the mire while struggling to keep up with their artillery barrages. Ground was taken, but it could not be held. In wretched conditions, with casualties mounting at an appalling rate, the Australians had to fall back. The troops were finally exhausted and could do no more; by the 15th of November, they handed over to the Canadians.

The Third Battle of Ypres was a bloodbath; 310,000 Allied casualties and an estimated 260,000 Germans.

After the Battle of Broodseinde, George, Sam, and Albert were rested along with the rest of the Australian 1st Division. They took the opportunity to make their way to Poperinge and reacquainted themselves with the delights of "Maison de Plaisir."

They also visited Tubby at Talbot House to reassure him they were all alive and reasonably well.

The Great War continued, and the 22nd Battalion was called back into action, all too soon in George's opinion.

They were ordered to march to Amiens, a fifty-mile march to join up with the rest of the Australian Corps.

'There's only one thing I hate more than German shells and gas. It's fucking marching with full pack for bloody miles,' Albert complained.

'I'm with you, cobber,' said Sam.

George had gone forward to receive their orders for the day and, upon returning, the look on his face showed his displeasure.

'Well, lads, don't get too comfortable. We're heading back north to Hazebrouck.'

'Where the fuck is Hazebrouck?' asked Sam.

'About twenty miles from Ypres.'

'Fuck, we've just marched fifty bloody miles south, and we have to turn around and march straight back,' complained Sam.

'There's no use complaining. We have to follow orders. We leave in thirty minutes.'

12 April 1918

The 1st Division arrived, weary and footsore, just in time to relieve the British who were exhausted from the fight. The 1st Division held a line eight miles from Hazebrouck, halting the German advance on the 13th and again on the 17th. The Germans abandoned their offensive, retreating back behind their lines at Messines.

The Invincibles survived another battle.

1918

CHAPTER 9

Hundred Days, 1918

The 1st Division returned to the Australian Corps on the 8th of August, 1918, the day on which the final British offensive commenced with the Battle of Amiens. The division was sent into action the following day, relieving the 5th Division, but arrived late owed to its rushed preparation. The 1st Division continued the attack for the next three days, driving towards Lihons, but progress was slow as the Australians moved beyond their supporting guns and tanks.

On the 23rd of August, the 1st Division attacked south of the River Somme towards Chuignes with the British 32nd Division on its southern flank, attacking Herleville. The Australians suffered one thousand casualties but took two thousand German prisoners out of a total of eight thousand captured by both the British Third and Fourth Armies on that day. The 1st also captured a German 15-in naval gun on 18 September, despite being severely depleted. Only two thousand eight hundred and fifty-four infantrymen out of division's twelve thousand two hundred and four nominal strength were available. The 1st Division took part in the assault on the Hindenburg "Outpost" Line during the Battle of Épehy, capturing a large section of the line.

After this, the division was withdrawn from the line. They would take no further part in the fighting, having lost six hundred and seventy-seven men in their final battle.

In early October, the rest of the Australian Corps, severely depleted due to heavy casualties and falling enlistments in Australia, was also withdrawn upon a request made by Prime Minister Billy Hughes, to reorganise in preparation for further operations On the 11th of November, an armistice came into effect, and as hostilities came to an end, the division's personnel were slowly repatriated back to Australia for demobilisation and discharge. This was completed by the 23rd of March, 1919, when the division was disbanded. Throughout the course of the war, the division suffered around fifteen thousand men killed and thirty-five thousand wounded, out of the eighty thousand men that served in its ranks.

Battles Fought by the Australian 1st Division

- Pozieres
- Mouquet Farm
- Le Barque
- Thilloy
- Boursies
- Demicourt
- Hermies
- Lagnicourt,
- Bullecourt
- Third Ypres
- Menin Road
- Broodseinde Ridge
- Poelcapelle
- Second Passchendaele
- Hazebrouck
- Somme
- Lihons
- Chuignolles
- Hindenburg Line
- Epehy

George, Sam and Albert survived them all, living up to the name they gave themselves, The Invincibles. They left behind three great cobbers Percy Smith, Dick Ruby and Mick Dwyer.

BLOODY BEWDY THE WAR'S OVER
CHAPTER 9

Early on the morning of the 10th of November, 1918, a messenger ran into the camp where the 1st Division had established its Headquarters, delivering an envelope to the Commander of the 1st Division, Major General Glasgow.

Glasgow read the message and remained silent as if absorbing the information and the implications it held for him and his men.

Glasgow walked outside, and found his second in command, Major Rhys.

'Major, come with me. I have something to discuss with you.'

'Yes, sir.'

The two men strode back to Glasgow's office.

'Sit down David. Can I pour you a Scotch, single malt 1901?'

'Well, sir, I wouldn't normally drink while on duty and certainly not at 11am, but...'

Major General Glasgow poured two generous glasses and handed one to his second in command.

'I would like to propose a toast, David.'

'Yes, sir.'

'To the end of this bloody war.'

'Well, I'll toast to that, and may it come soon.'

'David, it has. The war ends at 11am tomorrow.'

'Oh my God.'

'To be honest, I'm not sure God had anything to do with it.'

'I can't believe it! I've been fighting this war for three years, and now it's over.'

'I know how you feel, David. I've been fighting for four.'

'How should we communicate the good news to the men, sir?'

'I would like to gather the Battalion Leaders and they can convey the news to their men.'

Major David Rhys called together the BLs and informed them that the armistice would be signed at 11am on the 11th of November, 1918.

The mood was mixed. Some cheered while others looked perplexed, not knowing what would happen next.

The troops reacted in a similar manner. The war had been their life; their reason for their existence for the past four years.

After the armistice had been signed, the logistics of shipping home the Australian and New Zealand troops was a monumental task. General Monash became the leader responsible for getting the Australians home.

It would be some months before the last of the diggers returned home to a new life.

After the initial celebrations, George, Albert, and Sam had learned that they could enlist in several courses while they waited to be shipped home. The one course that interested them all was learning how to weld. Welding was a fairly new technology and would be very useful on the farm for fixing equipment. They agreed they should enrol in this course being conducted on the outskirts of Paris and when this was completed, they could spend some time getting to know Paris and, with luck, some of the Parisian women.

They had all registered their interest in the Soldier Land Settlement Program before the war ended and all indications were that they would be successful.

The three prospective farmers completed the course, all passing without too many problems.

They then moved to central Paris and booked rooms at a little hotel in The Marais in the 4th arrondissement. They chose this area based on a recommendation of a French sergeant they got to know in Poperinge. His recommendation was made on the basis it was close to many attractions they had intended to visit, including the Eiffel Tower.

They also were looking forward to experiencing Paris's famous nightspots and the red light district of Montmartre.

Paris during the war became drab and the citizens despondent; the gaiety of the French capital had deserted it. News of battles such as Verdun and The Somme and the horrendous casualties suffered only made the mood of the city darker. One saving grace was that Germany didn't target Paris in concentrated bombing raids as they did with London. A single Taube reconnaissance aircraft did drop bombs on every trip it made over the city of lights, though; fifty in all. Notre Dame Cathedral suffered some damage.

Once the war had been declared officially over and her sons returned home, the city went back to the Paris of old. Restaurants and cafés were again overflowing, mainly with American soldiers but also soldiers from Australia and New Zealand.

The famous Paris cabarets reopened except for the most famous of all. The *Moulin Rouge* had burned down in 1915. These venues were very popular with the troops, as were the Paris brothels such as Le Chabanais.

The other major event taking place near Paris was more serious. It was termed "The Paris Peace Conference."

The Paris Peace Conference was the meeting of the Allied victors, following the end of World War 1, to set the peace terms for the defeated Central Powers following the armistices of 1918. It took place in Paris during 1919 and involved diplomats from more than thirty-two countries and nationalities. The major decisions were the creation of the League of Nations; the five peace treaties with defeated enemies, including the Treaty of Versailles with Germany; the awarding of German and Ottoman overseas possessions as "mandates", chiefly to Britain and France; reparations imposed on Germany, and the drawing of new national boundaries (sometimes with plebiscites) to better reflect the forces of nationalism. The main result was the Treaty of Versailles, with Germany, which in section 231 laid the guilt for the war on "the aggression of Germany and her allies." This provision proved humiliating for Germany, and set the stage for very high reparations Germany was supposed to pay.

Versailles Hall of Mirrors

The beauty of Paris and its vibrancy overwhelmed the young Aussie diggers as they wandered around the tree-lined boulevards. The first museum they visited was The Louvre. Everybody had heard of the Mona Lisa, even these boys from a far away land. They were a little disappointed to find the painting so small. They'd imagined a painting much like the other large

70

paintings hung on the walls of the famous museum. Still, they enjoyed their visit; particularly Napoleon's apartment.

'More like a bloody palace than an apartment if you ask me,' commented Albert.

'Yep, I think I could be very comfortable living here. Where's Josephine when you need her?' said Sam.

'I can just imagine Josephine sitting on the little general's lap on that throne,' said George.

Napoleon's Throne

'Come on, we've got a lot more to see this afternoon,' he added. 'Where do you want to go next, mate?'

'There's a place up the river a bit called the "Concierge". It's where they kept the prisoners before they cut their heads off. Apparently, it was where Marie Antoinette spent her last days.'

'Geez mate, that sounds a bit macabre, especially with what we've been through and seen in the last few years,' said Sam.

'Don't be silly, Sam. It's fucking history, just like the bloody war. You'll have all sorts of people analysing what went right and what went wrong in the years to come.'

'All right, let's go and see a French bloody prison. I'm looking forward to tonight when we go to Montmartre.'

The three mates started off down the pathway running beside the Seine to visit the Concierge.

Concierge During Revolution

They joined a tour through the magnificent building, including the cells below. They saw the cell where the barber cut the victims' hair to ensure a clean cut. They also viewed Marie's cell where she and her children were kept before being taken to meet Madam Guillotine.

'Okay, that's enough history for one day. I suggest we walk over to the soldiers' club Captain Hill told us about. Miss Butler's place… apparently she's English and established the club so that our soldiers could relax and drink coffee or tea,' said George.

'Sounds good to me. I'm a bit knackered,' said Sam.

'Me too. Let's go,' agreed Albert.

They strolled down to 19 Place Vendome and entered the building, to be greeted by Miss Butler herself.

'Welcome, boys! Australians are always welcome here. Go inside and find yourselves a table.'

'Thank you, madam.'

The three Aussies entered the magnificent lounge and three French women summoned them over to their table.

'Messieurs souhaitez-vous vous joindre à nous à notre table?'

'What did she say, George?' asked Sam.

'She asked us whether we would care to join them.'

'Well, say yes. They're beautiful,' Sam enthused.

'Oui Madame, nous serions honorés de vous rejoindre.'

The three men sat at the table and introduced themselves as best they could in French.

The blonde girl, Fleur, explained there was no need to try to speak French as they could all speak English.

Sam went bright red.

'No need to feel embarrassed, Sam. It was a very nice thing to say.

They ordered tea and pastries and conversed with the three young ladies for an hour or two before they excused themselves to go back to the hotel. They did arrange to see Danique, Fleur and Marguerite again on Saturday.

The Australians walked back to their accommodation, Hotel Du Vieux Saule, a small hotel housed in a sixteenth-century building. They bathed and changed into their freshly laundered uniforms ready to experience the red light district of Montmartre.

George suggested they take the Metro, the underground rail system, which was initially opened in time for the world fair in 1900.

None of them had ridden in a train before they arrived in France, let alone one that travelled underground, so they were fascinated.

It wasn't long before they arrived at Montmartre Station where they climbed the stairs and the red light district in all her glory was there to greet them. The coloured lights the servicemen saw everywhere made for an exciting atmosphere. What made it even more exciting were the French whores standing on the street corners plying their trade.

The lads had decided when they were fighting in the trenches that, if they survived, they would visit the most famous and expensive brothel in Paris.

George asked an American Marine where they could find 12, Rue Chabanais, and the American gave them a wink and directions.

George, being the leader of the group, knocked on the door.

A beautiful young woman in an evening gown greeted them and showed them in.

'So you are here to be with one of my girls?'

'Yes, madam, the thought of visiting your fine establishment kept us going when we were fighting in the war.'

'This is good. Please follow me to the lounge and you can choose which lady you would like to be with.'

The three soldiers followed her into a very ornate lounge area where there were several ladies to greet them.

Their jaws dropped, for in front of them were several half-naked ladies just waiting to be chosen by the Australian diggers.

After much discussion within the group, they chose a lady each. It was now time to pay the Madam. In Pops, the fee was two and a half francs for thirty minutes and five for the hour.

Le Chabanais's fee was five francs for thirty minutes or ten for the hour. The boys didn't mind. They had plenty of money and this, they believed, would be a once in a lifetime opportunity.

Each was taken by the hand by the beautiful mademoiselle he had chosen and led to the magnificent bedrooms.

After an hour, they all met back in the lounge. All three were beaming.

Once outside in the street, they all began to laugh and hit each other on the arm.

'How fucking good was that?' said George.

'Pretty fucking good,' said Sam.

'What about you, Albert?'

'The best I've ever had.'

'Let's go and get a drink.'

'Bloody good idea,' said Albert.

The contented soldiers headed for their favourite drinking hole, the Café Charbon in the Latin Quarter, close to their hotel.

They all ordered German beer.

'As much as I hated the bloody Germans when we were fighting them, I like their beer,' said Sam.

'So, what are we going to do tomorrow, fellas?' asked George.

'I don't think we could top today,' said Sam.

'Do you want to go to another museum?'

'I think I've had enough of museums for the moment,' said Albert.

'Well, why don't we just walk the streets and check out the Champs Elysees and all that sort of stuff,' said George.

It was agreed. The Australians finished their beers and headed back to their hotel for a well-earned sleep.

SOLDIERS' LAND SETTLEMENT SCHEME

This booklet was originated in the interest of the Soldier Settlement Scheme. Its mission is to place at the Soldier's disposal sufficient information governing his requirements to commence farming in Western Canada. There will no doubt be many helpful suggestions offered him, but *T. EATON C⁰. has given this subject careful attention for over a year, as we anticipated such a scheme being brought forward.
It is necessary, in catering to a great scheme of this kind, that provision be made for the necessary supply of goods and supplying them immediately, so that the soldiers are not hampered in carrying out their arrangements. It is also essential that they be not loaded up with supplies they do not require for immediate use. With this idea in view *T. EATON C⁰. originated and published this booklet advising the Soldier just what he might require to commence with. Should he require more, he has the privilege of adding to it according to his requirements, but he is safe-guarded from an over supply when he deals through our Company.

WHAT THIS BOOKLET CONTAINS

In this booklet you will find four different Soldier equipments, as follows:
Equipment No. 1, One-Man Equipment, including House Type A.
Equipment No. 2, Two or Three-Man Equipment, including House Type B.
Equipment No. 3, for man, wife and small family, including House Type C.
Equipment No. 4, for man, wife and larger family, including House Type D.
It contains official plans and drawings of buildings which have been designed by the Settlement Board, for Soldier Settlers use only, for their farms. It gives illustrations of suggested house furnishings, machinery, harness, wagons, etc., quoting prices of each. This information should be of valuable assistance to the Soldier who might or might not be well acquainted with his necessities. The greatest feature of this booklet is that it deals with the full requirements of the Soldier, this being possible on account of our big Store handling practically every line of goods he will need (except live-stock). In using this booklet and following its suggestions, every Canadian Soldier is assured of straightforward treatment, secured by the EATON guarantee, and also that no transaction is complete until the Soldier is satisfied.

COMPARE OUR GOODS AND PRICES

The Soldier will, no doubt, be confronted with a great many propositions. The Government will endeavor to assist him from every point of view. Service is also a great factor in a scheme of this kind. *T. EATON C⁰. has been in business a great many years, and has built its present business on a price-and-service basis. We can assure you that our Company is not in a position to offer discounts, because the original pricing would not allow it, as we depend on our great turn-over for our profits. When you are making your choice as to where you intend to buy your equipment, we suggest that you see the goods and compare the prices before purchasing. Our IMPERIAL line of implements and Soldiers' equipments will stand closest inspection, and the price will stand comparison without special discounts being offered. We also have at our disposal the greatest service any store in Canada ever had. This service cannot be bought—it is given away to customers doing business with us. You have the privilege of leaving with us the loading of your cars, the packing and shipping of your goods, the careful consideration of all your needs, and the despatch of the goods on time. Even then our responsibilities do not cease. We ensure their delivery to you just as complete as you ordered them. If the goods are broken or missing we replace them without any delay. If the whole shipment is lost we duplicate it? This service does practically all the work for you. The Soldier may make his selection from this booklet, or our big general catalogue, or call upon us personally in our implement room, select his requirements, pay his money, and we will do the rest.

EATON SERVICE

We have a fine, big implement room in Winnipeg, and we have big display rooms at our warehouses at Regina and Saskatoon. In these display rooms you see every implement you wish to purchase. Check it over carefully and make your comparisons with others. You can gather data and information from our experts, as we have experts in practically every line.
Our Harness is made in our own EATON Factories, carefully inspected, for when we advertise specifications they mean exactly what is stated. Our leathers are purchased by experts who know leather, and it is not their intention to make a cheap harness. It is their ambition to make a serviceable harness which will give satisfaction.
Our large Mail Order System will give you a quick, efficient service, so by using it you are assured of the same careful attention as though you were making your purchases personally.
We have opened a Soldiers' Settlement Department, which will handle all Soldiers' equipment orders we receive. Therefore, when writing or sending in an order, address your envelope to

PRICES QUOTED IN THIS BOOK REMAIN IN EFFECT UNTIL JULY 30th, 1919	ᵀᴴᴱ T. EATON C⁰. LIMITED WINNIPEG SASKATOON REGINA Soldiers' Settlement Department	PRICES QUOTED IN THIS BOOK REMAIN IN EFFECT UNTIL JULY 30th, 1919

SOLDIERS' FARM EQUIPMENT No. 1

The merchandise described below comprises the Soldiers' Land Settlement Equipment No. 1. This equipment is suggested for the man who intends to go on the land alone, and who therefore requires a good, strong and substantial outfit.

ONE-MAN EQUIPMENT

HOUSE, Type "A"—Designed by Soldier Settlement Board. (For illustration see page 17.)

Size 14 ft. by 17 ft. 10 in., with 8 ft. stud with 9 ft. 6 in. ceiling, consisting of living-room, bedroom and small vestibule. Provision is also made for clothes closet off bedroom and a place to hang hats and coats in vestibule.
This house is to be constructed on cedar posts set in ground below frost line on pad stone or other suitable base. On top of these posts wall plates consisting of two pieces 2x10 placed on edge for the joists to rest on. All framing is placed at 18-inch centres. A double floor is provided, the sheathing of the building is of rabbeted jointed shiplap covered with Government standard flint coated ready roofing in two colors, laid on weather-tight. This material, with a liberal use of building paper, as specified, will make a wind-tight job.
The interior is finished with Wall Board, pleasingly panelled with wood strips. The walls are finished with neat base board to floor, and all openings are trimmed. A concrete chimney is to be built according to the Government specifications. Storm sash and combination doors for Winter protection are provided, and window screens are included for Summer use. This building is designed to use standard size materials and stock articles without ornamentation, but all being perfectly neat and plain. Any man who understands carpentry should be able to erect this building complete in six days, exclusive of any concrete work.
Should you desire at some further date to enlarge your building, this house will not be wasted but just added to, which will form type "B," and later on if desired a further addition will form type "C" house.

Price and Detailed Specification supplied by Soldier Settlement Board.

BARN—Designed by Soldier Settlement Board. (For illustration see page 17.)

Size 12 ft. by 24 ft., lean-to style, accommodating four horses and two cattle. Height 9 ft. in front, 8 ft. at rear.
A very convenient barn for the settler who requires this accommodation. The stalls are divided with 2-inch plank partition, and 2-inch plank material is supplied for mangers.
The whole building is to be set on ties or pad stones, to form a good foundation. The studs and rafters are spaced at 18-inch centres, making a substantial building for the purposes intended. All materials are supplied, and no difficulty will be experienced in erecting this barn. Three to four days should be sufficient time for any man handy with carpentry tools. Ample light and ventilation is provided for, and a small manure door at the end of litter way is very convenient for cleaning out.
The Government specifications call for dependable lumber. The barn will be roofed with Government standard flint coated ready roofing.

Price and Detailed Specification supplied by Soldier Settlement Board.

*T. EATON C⁰. LIMITED
WINNIPEG SASKATOON
REGINA   PRICES QUOTED IN THIS BOOK REMAIN IN EFFECT UNTIL JULY 30th, 1919

1

'Hey George, what do you think about this; the Government wants to settle us all on our own farms.'

'Bullshit. The Government doesn't give anything away. They just take.'

Reverend Tubby Clayton overheard their conversation and approached them.

'Excuse me, boys do you mind if I join the conversation? I might be able to explain a few things.'

'Come join us, Reverend. We'd be grateful for your input,' George said.

'Apparently each individual state has committed to allocating Crown land and acquiring existing farms to be allocated to returning soldiers if they wish to become farmers.'

'Why in the… why would they want to do that, Reverend?'

'Please call me Tubby. Everybody else does. They recognise the enormous sacrifice you are making fighting for our country. This is the country's way of saying thank you.'

'Well I'll be; you know what? I used to work on my father-in-law's cane farm in Queensland. I'd certainly be interested,' said Albert enthusiastically.

'The key is "returning soldiers". We've got a way to go in this bloody war before we qualify as a returned soldier. If you could just tell the Germans we're all keen to be farmers, Tubby, we sure would appreciate not being killed,' George said with a sarcastic tone.

'George, I get your meaning. You have just got to have faith.'

'Easier said than done, Tubby. When you've seen what we've seen over the past eighteen months or so it's pretty hard to keep your faith.'

'I understand, George. I've also seen the horrors of war, but it's the only thing we've got to cling to. Somehow, it's God's way.'

A French Experience
Chapter 10

'What time are we meeting the ladies?' asked Albert.

'They suggested we meet them at Miss Butler's at six pm,' answered George.

All three went to their rooms and were asleep as soon as their heads touched the pillows. They woke next morning and went down to the breakfast room at nine am.

The day was spent walking the streets and boulevards of Paris and having lunch in a small café on The Rue de Rivoli.

Returning to the hotel late afternoon, they changed clothes and met in the foyer ready to walk the three blocks to Miss Butler's place.

They walked into the lounge and chose a table for six. The expectant diggers waited for forty-five minutes but the ladies hadn't arrived.

'Do you think they're gunna show up, George?' asked Sam.

'Who knows, mate. It's not looking too promising, I must admit.'

'How long do you reckon we should wait?' asked Albert.

'Let's give them another quarter hour. If they don't show up by then, fuck em.'

Just at that moment, Danique, Fleur and Marguerite walked into the lounge. They all looked absolutely stunning. The boys stood up and pulled out the chairs for their escorts.

'We were worried we had the wrong day, ladies,' said George.

'We must apologise. We got held up.'

'Well, it was certainly worth the wait. You all look beautiful.'

'Thank you.'

'Well, ladies, it's your city… where do you suggest we go for dinner?'

'We have a little surprise for you boys. We have prepared a traditional French meal at our apartment not far from where we are now,' said Fleur.

'That's why we were running late,' said Marguerite.

'Well, that sounds wonderful.'

The group left Miss Butler's and strode along the boulevard until they reached 16 Rue de Brosse where they climbed the steps to the third floor.

Danique unlocked the door and entered, beckoning the others to follow.

The Australians were flabbergasted; the apartment was like something out of a magazine, being large with magnificent furniture and large gold gilded mirrors.

'This is magnificent, ladies; I can't believe it,' said George.

'We're glad you like it. Come and have a look at the view from the balcony.'

The view was of the River Seine and the buildings lining it including the Louvre.

'Please sit down and relax. Would you like a glass of champagne?'

The boys accepted. Having never tasted champagne before, they were not sure what to expect.

Fleur produced a bottle of Dom Perignon and asked George to pour it.

George had no idea how to pour champagne; as a result, it spilled over the top of the glass.

'George you pour champagne the same way you pour beer, tilt the glass and pour it slowly,' Fleur advised.

'I'm sorry, Fleur. I've never tried pouring champagne before. In fact, I've never even tasted it.'

'Don't worry, George, we were all champagne virgins at one stage in our lives,' she said, giggling.

'So boys— what have you been doing in Paris since we met you?' asked Danique.

The three men gave a full account of their Parisian activities except for their visit to Le Chabanais.

'May I ask you all how long you have lived in this magnificent apartment?' asked Albert.

'I was born here,' answered Fleur. 'My parents lived here for many years. Mother died when I was sixteen, so my father raised me.'

'Where is your father now?' asked George.

'He was a General in the army but he died during the Battle of Verdun. I miss him terribly.'

'Oh, I am sorry to hear that, Fleur.'

'Very sad, but life must go on. Let's not speak of that anymore; can I ask you to follow me into the dining room so we can experience what the other ladies have prepared for us?'

Danique and Marguerite had prepared Fleur's favourite dish, Duck a l'Orange, brought to the table on an antique silver platter.

To accompany the main course, Fleur had chosen Montrachet Chardonnay and Romanee-Conti Burgundy from her father's extensive wine cellar.

The three Aussie diggers felt right out of their depth as the most exotic meal they had ever eaten was a lamb roast for Sunday dinner.

Marguerite sensed their unease.

'Don't feel like a duck out of water as it were, gentlemen. We are putting on this dinner as a thank you for all that you have done for our beloved France. We simply ask you to enjoy the food and the wine.'

George, Sam, and Albert tucked into the duck, enjoying every morsel; they had never tasted wine like what was being served with the meal. Overall, it was magnificent dinner.

The conversation flowed around the table, mainly answering the ladies' questions about life in Australia, and their future plans when they returned home.

Fleur disappeared into the kitchen, returning a short while later with dessert, a profiterole tower. The boys had never seen anything like it.

After dessert, a suggestion was made by Fleur to return to the sitting room where they could all partake in a coffee and cognac.

This was another new experience for the diggers as they hadn't even heard of cognac before, let alone 100-year-old Courvoisier L'Esprit.

Towards the end of the evening, Fleur rose and approached Sam. She held out her hand and led him to her bedroom.

The other ladies followed Fleur's lead; Marguerite chose George and Albert and Danique were the final pair.

When morning came, the six lovers shared a breakfast of croissants, jam and coffee.

The three ladies bade their Australian lovers farewell. It would be the last they all saw of one another as the soldiers received their orders next day; they were being shipped home.

GOING HOME
CHAPTER 11

August 1919

The Battalions of the Australian 1st Division were shipped from France to England where they boarded their ship home; *HMAT Khyber*.

HMAT Khyber

The voyage would take two months through some very rough seas, where half the passengers on board suffered seasickness.

George and his two mates were allocated a hammock below deck. It was hot and stuffy during the day, especially when they were in the Middle East. They tried to get up on deck as much as possible, and they even resorted to sleeping on the deck at night. It was freezing cold, making sleep difficult and very uncomfortable. Conditions weren't much better down below.

Things were about to get worse. Spanish Flu had been detected among the troops.

Spanish Flu

Spanish Flu hit the world in the summer of 1918, as the Great War was ending with the death rate approaching twenty million people.

When Spanish Flu disappeared in 1919, it had claimed between seventy and one hundred million people.

In today's terms, that would equate to one hundred and sixty million killed, including civilians, through war, and four hundred and sixty-six million dying resulting from Spanish Flu.

No one really knows where Spanish Flu began. Some say China; others, the Middle East. There is also conjecture as to why it was called Spanish Flu. Again, some say because of the high mortality rate in Spain, while others say it was that Spain was neutral and therefore had a free press which could report what was really happening.

The pandemic eventually had a disastrous effect on the Germans and their allies, inflicting massive casualties through sickness which they could ill afford as the British and its allies were having significant success on the battlefield.

The virus spread across the Atlantic to the USA via the military convoys. Many died on the ships as the symptoms were a brief fever followed by death. The virus caused uncontrollable haemorrhaging that filled the lungs, and patients would drown in their own blood.

The reasons for the pandemic essentially remain unknown. The deprivations of a world war are held responsible by some scientists, although the virus similarly swept through non-war affected countries like the USA, India and much of Europe.

For example, four hundred and fifty thousand civilian deaths occurred in the United States. Most deaths were in the twenty to forty age groups. In Britain, some two hundred and twenty-eight thousand civilians died and four hundred thousand in Germany. Hardest hit, however, was India with a reported sixteen million casualties alone.

Each nation at war went to great lengths to conceal the extent of losses suffered through the virus, concerned that such reports would serve to encourage their enemies. In reality, each was suffering as badly as the other.

Curiously, in mid-1919 the pandemic withered and died abruptly without a treatment having been found. Scientists continue to believe that a repeat of the pandemic, albeit in a varying form, would find science equally unprepared to meet its challenge.

'What's all this panic about Spanish Flu, George? I've never even been to fucking Spain. All I know about the place is bull fighting and blokes wearing really tight trousers and ridiculous hats.'

'I'm not sure, Sam, but the officers seem pretty concerned, I'm not sure why; I've had the flu before. A couple of days in bed and you're up and about again; good as gold.

The Invincibles began to understand the severity of it all when two diggers contracted a cold and then started to get the symptoms of the flu. Twenty-four hours later, they were lying in the ship's morgue.

'I don't get this, those two blokes who died, Harry and Will, were bloody good soldiers. I think Harry won the Military Medal at Pozières. They've been with us at Gallipoli and the Western Front and survived. Now they've been taken out by the poxy flu five weeks from getting home after four years away; how in the fuck does that work?' said Albert.

'I don't bloody know. What I do know, is I'm staying well clear of any bastard who sneezes or coughs,' said Sam.

'I'm with you, Sam. I didn't enlist to fight for my country and put up with hell for all these years only to cark it on a rusty bloody ship on my way home,' said George.

There were very few surgical masks on board to help limit the spread of the deadly virus, so the troops were instructed to use a clean handkerchief as a makeshift mask.

By the time the *Khyber* reached Freemantle in Western Australia, more than three hundred cases had been reported. Commonwealth immigration authorities initially refused to allow the soldiers to disembark, as there had been no cases reported in Western Australia thus far.

The authorities finally agreed to let three hundred of the most unwell diggers to be ferried ashore to the quarantine station at Woodman Point south of Freemantle. Many more soldiers died at the station over the following week.

To further exacerbate the dire situation, more than twenty medical staff became infected.

Meanwhile, on board ship where most of the men remained, conditions were said to be deplorable. A seven-day incubation period with no new cases was required to prove that the disease had burned itself out, but new infections and deaths continued, caused by the cramped and close living conditions.

Public outrage grew against the refusal of the immigration authorities to allow all the soldiers ashore with casualties growing each day. Wrangling between the State Minister for Health and the Federal immigration authorities continued, and tensions increased to the point that the RSL made threats to storm the ship to return the sick men to shore.

After nine days of acrimony, and despite breaking quarantine regulations, the ship was ordered to depart, in an attempt to defuse the volatile situation.

Another seventeen cases were discovered en route to Adelaide; consequently, the remaining men were disembarked at Torrens Island quarantine station. No further deaths occurred, and after being given clearance, the remaining men returned to their homes. A total of twenty-seven soldiers and four nurses at Woodman Point, WA, died of influenza during the crisis.

This was not the welcome home George, Sam, and Albert were expecting, but they remained free from the deadly virus.

The *Khyber* sailed on to Melbourne where they finally disembarked. George was back in his home state; Sam sailed to Hobart, in Tasmania and Albert to Townsville in Queensland.

GEE IT'S GOOD TO BE BACK HOME
CHAPTER 11

George said farewell to his mates and promised to keep in touch. They had been to hell and back together and friendships like that should continue forever.

George was met at Prince's Wharf by his mother and father and his two younger sisters; they could be seen all waving as their hero disembarked down the gangway. George ran to his family, giving his mother a huge hug and his father a firm handshake. His father grabbed his arm. That would be the closest his father would get to demonstrate affection to his only son.

The two girls, Lila and Vida, hugged and kissed him and wouldn't let go of their hero.

They all walked down to where Roy had parked the Bullnose Morris and climbed aboard.

'Well Dad… this is new! You were riding a bicycle when I left.'

'You've got to get with the times, George. Best investment I ever made.'

'How's work going, Dad?'

'It's pretty good although with the war ending business has dropped off.'

'Gee, if I'd know the war was good for business I would have tried to keep it going for a bit longer.'

Roy just looked at his son with a half-smile on his face. 'You haven't changed much, son. Just as cheeky as ever.'

The family arrived home to their terrace in Fitzroy and walked inside. George entered the living room to find thirty odd friends and family with a banner "Welcome Home George" strewn across the room. It was the last thing he expected or really wanted.

There were lots of kisses and handshakes with the mandatory, 'What was it really like over there?'

George's answer was, 'Oh, it wasn't too bad.' What he would have liked to say was, 'Oh, it wasn't too bad considering we were living in a ditch most of the time up to our knees in mud with rats scampering around eating the corpses of our dead mates and the fucking Germans were shooting at us without reprieve.'

Eventually, the guests left the house and George could relax a little with his immediate family.

His father offered him a whisky, which was gladly accepted.

'I know it's early days, son, but have you thought about what you might like to do with your life?'

'Yeah, Dad. I have thrown around a few ideas.'

'You know you're quite welcome to join me in the butchery.'

'Thanks, Dad, but it's not really what I want to do.'

'So what options do you have?'

'I'm thinking seriously about taking up the Government's Land Settlement Program. You know, get a farm and work it until you can make a good living out of it.'

'That sounds all very fine, George, but you know nothing about farming. Who's going to teach you?'

'It can't be that hard. You plough the soil, plant some wheat seed, watch it grow then harvest it.'

'Yeah, sounds like a piece of cake, George. So when are you going to become farmer? And where's the farm?'

'I've already registered with The Closer Settlement Board. I am being interviewed next week, and all going well, I should be working on my own farm inside three months.'

'What the hell is The Closer Settlement Board? It sounds like inner city living to me.'

'Yeah, it does, a bit. They're responsible for allocating the land and granting you a sum of money for living and buying equipment. They also organise training initially.'

'What, they sit you down in a classroom and teach you farming?'

'No, some bloke who's an expert comes out to the farm and analyses what you've got and what improvements need to be made. Training is also given on proper farming practices.'

'You haven't told me where the farm is, mate.'

'I don't know until they approve my application. It could be anywhere.'

'So let me get this right… they give you a farm and give you money to equip it, then they pay you a wage while you get it up and going?'

'Not exactly, Dad. They lend you the money to buy the farm with a low-interest loan.'

'I thought it sounded too good to be true. What interest rate are they going to charge you?'

'Initially three and a half per cent, then they whack it up half a percent each year until it reaches the commercial rate. By that time I'll be making plenty to cover it.'

'You hope.'

'Dad, I thought you'd be happy for me. Here's my chance to be independent and do something with my life.'

'Don't get me wrong, George. I am happy for you. I'm just worried it may not work out. If it doesn't, you know I would welcome you as a partner in the butchery.'

'It'll work out.'

For the interview, George donned his best suit… actually it was his only suit. His father lent him a white shirt and a striped tie. His favourite hat completed the outfit; one he wore before the war.

The tram to the city where the offices of the Qualification Committee were located stopped outside his parents' front door. The prospective farmer would arrive in Exhibition Street nice and early.

George entered the foyer where a rather pretty receptionist sat behind the counter.

'Hello, miss, my name is George Harris. I have an appointment with the Qualification Committee at two pm.'

'Take a seat, Mr Harris. The committee will see you shortly.'

George sat down on the dark wood bench seat and looked around at the offices. They were dark wood panelled with a large ornate almost gothic window at the end of the room. It reminded George of a church but without the stained glass windows.

The door at the far end of the room opened, and a bloke George knew walked out all smiles.

'G'day George. Are you going to be a farmer too?'

'I hope so, Harry. You look as if you've just won the lottery. I suspect you've been approved.'

'Yep, don't know where I'm getting my block, but they told me I'm approved.'

'Good on you, Harry, I hope I'll be joining you.'

'Good luck mate. I don't think you have to worry, what with your war record and all.'

'Thanks, mate. I hope I do all right.'

The large door at the end of the room opened, and an elderly gentleman called George's name.

Harry gave George a nod and left.

George walked up to the man. They shook hands and George was invited to sit at the long board table.

There were five other gentlemen seated opposite and one man, who must have been the committee chairman, asked the first question.

'Mr Harris, your rank of corporal was awarded to you in the field. Why do you think you were promoted?'

'I think I was seen to have leadership qualities, and I had demonstrated I could fight, sir.'

'Good answer, Mr Harris. Do you have any farming experience at all?'

'Sir, my father is a butcher I have worked with him throughout my life. We often visited farms to examine livestock, and I worked on several farms during school holidays.'

'I take it these were sheep and cattle farms?'

'Yes, also wheat farms that ran livestock.'

'Do you drink alcohol, Mr Harris?'

'Very rarely, sir.'

'Excellent. We have read your character references and they are also excellent.

'Just one more question. Are you married?'

'I'm engaged, sir.'

'When are you getting married?'

'We haven't set a date yet. It really depends on whether I get approved.'

'Well, George, I think you can go home and arrange that wedding day.'

'Does that mean I'm approved?'

'Yes, George. Congratulations.'

'Thank you sir! Thanks to all of you.'

'We will consider the best location for your experience and skills, and you'll receive a letter in the next week or so. Congratulations again. I'm sure you will become a very successful farmer.'

George left the boardroom, thanked the receptionist, and skipped down the stairs into the street. The returned soldier was on top of the world. Catching the tram home and unable to contain his excitement, George couldn't wait to tell his family the good news.

Opening the front door, George yelled, 'I'm in! They accepted my application. Hello, is anybody home, I'm going farming.'

Unfortunately, there was nobody home, so he had to contain his excitement until the family was together at the dinner table.

George decided to go over the road to his good mate Frank who had also recently returned from fighting in the Middle East.

Knocking on the door, hoping Frank was home, he was relieved to be called to come in.

'Hey, Frankie, I just got accepted for the Soldier Settlement Program.'

'Well done, mate! Where are you going to be farming?'

'Fucked if I know, they reckon I'll get a letter in the next week or so.'

'Are they going to train you on how to be a farmer? Let's face it Georgie, you know fuck all about farming.'

'You sound like Dad. They train you up on all the ins and outs and some bloke who knows what it's all about comes and visits the farm regularly. It can't be that hard; it's not medicine.'

'Yeah, I suppose you're right… it can't be all that hard.'

'What about you, Frankie? Have you decided what you're going to do?'

'To be honest, I don't know. I've thought about going back to the bank as there's a job waiting for me there, but it doesn't really appeal. The war has changed me a bit… well actually, a lot. The thought of being a teller again doesn't really do it for me.'

'Why don't you become a farmer like me? You're out in the open air, with no fucking boss to report to, and you can make a bloody good living.'

'I have thought about that, but I know nothing about it. Having said that, listening to you makes me think maybe I should give it a go.'

'Good on you, mate. I can fill you in on the questions they'll probably ask you. By the way, I told a porky about being engaged. The board members prefer married men, so I suggest you do the same.'

'Thanks mate. I'll let you know how I go.'

'Okay, I'd better get going. The folks should be home by now.'

'See ya, George.'

George returned home just in time for dinner.

His father sat down, asking, 'Well son, out with it, how do you think you went?'

'Pretty good, Dad. I've been accepted.'

'Congratulations! When do you leave?'

'They'll let me know in a week or so.'

'Did they tell you what region you'll be going to?'

'Not yet.'

As the family ate their dinner of bangers and mash, George's mother, Elsie, was unusually quiet.

'Are you okay, Mum? You're not saying much.' George said.

'It's just that we get you home after four years of fighting not knowing whether you were alive from one day to the next and you're no sooner home than you tell us you are going away into the country somewhere, and we won't see you much again.'

'Mum, it's not as though I'll be halfway across the world. I'll be a regular visitor, I'm sure and I'd love for the family to visit me on the farm. I'll make sure I build a farmhouse with enough bedrooms for you all.'

'George, are you going to grow sheep? I love sheep,' Vida put in.

'I don't know yet, Vi, but I would like some.'

'What about cows?' asked Lila.

'Maybe.'

'Well. I'm really excited for you, George. I'm looking forward to visiting you down on the farm,' enthused Lila.

'Me too,' agreed Vida.

A letter arrived ten days after the interview confirming George had been accepted as a participant in the Soldier Settlement Program.

Two hundred acres had been granted at a place called Mt Violet in the Western District.

Suggested use was sheep grazing.

How About Them Apples?
Chapter 12

Sam's ship, the Aurora, berthed at Hobart wharf on a Saturday afternoon. Sam looked out over the sea of people waiting to greet the diggers home, looking for the familiar faces of his family. He hadn't seen them in over four years.

There were just too many people. Sam couldn't recognise anyone. What he didn't know was his mother, father, and little sister Jane could see him. They were waving and yelling his name, but Sam was oblivious to their presence.

It came time for him to disembark. Sam strode down the gangplank and began to walk through the crowd looking for his family. Finally, the familiar sound of his father's voice was heard. He looked over to see them all shouting and waving. Sam hurried over to them and hugged his mother; his sister Jane hugged him from behind at the same time. Eventually, he turned to his father, Roy. He held out his hand, but Roy pulled his son to him and gave him a mighty hug. They all had tears in their eyes, and it was the first time Sam had seen his father cry.

'Right Sam, let's get away from this bedlam and get you home,' said Roy.

They all walked up to Murray Street where Roy had parked his new Model T.

'Nice car, Dad. How long have you had it?'

'Only got it a month ago; she drives like a dream.'

The drive along the Huon Road took them past Mount Wellington, which had a dusting of snow, and through the rain forests before they reached Huonville two hours later.

Sam asked about the local news and what had been happening in the valley while he had been away.

His father informed him that of the sixty men who enlisted from the valley, fifteen had been killed. Sam had had no idea so many valley men had lost their lives in that horrible bloody war.

The remainder of the trip was taken up by the local gossip, including who had died and who had got married etc.

Once they entered the federation house, Elsie made tea and brought out the scones she had baked that morning.

At last, they could start asking Sam the questions they had been dying to ask.

'Well son, it must be good to be home?' said Roy.

'Sure is Dad, there were times I thought I would never get back here.'

'What was it really like, Sam?' asked Jane.

'Not very good Jane; not good at all. Don't get me wrong, the mateship was great, and we did have some good times but they were few and far between.'

'Did you kill many Germans?'

'Jane, don't ask such horrible questions,' her mother said.

'Well, he was in the war for four years so he must have killed lots.'

'That's enough, Jane.'

'It's all right Mum; I can understand Jane's curiosity. Jane, war is horrible. It's not glorious. Men on both sides lose their lives and their families back home have to cope with that, just as you would've had to if I had died. I don't want to talk about the details to anyone so let's just leave it at that.'

'Right, that's that, let's get onto more positive things; have you decided what you might like to do now, son?' asked his father.

'I've applied for a land grant under the Soldier Settlement Program. I'm hoping I get an orchard down here in the valley.'

'You don't know anything about growing apples, Sam. How are you going to learn and make a living at the same time? I know the police force are looking for recruits why don't you apply?'

'I don't want to be a policeman, Dad. As much as I respect you and what you do, I believe with hard work I can make a real go at being an orchardist.'

'Well, it's your choice son, and you have obviously made up your mind.'

'I have to get through the selection process first so who knows, if I don't get through I'll join the police force.'

'When will you know?'

'I got a letter the other day while I was in Melbourne. It was from the Soldier Settlement Committee and I'm required to be interviewed in Hobart on Thursday next week.'

For his interview, Sam dressed in his best double-breasted suit and borrowed a tie from his father.

Roy offered to drive him. Sam was grateful as it would have taken him half the day to get to Hobart under his own steam. Roy let him out on the corner of Argyle and Davey streets, about a block from where Sam needed to go.

Walking up to the committee's offices, Sam rehearsed his answers to the possible questions they were likely to ask. One question had him stumped was, 'Are you married?' Sam had a long-term relationship with his sweetheart Jessie, and in all probability, they would be married. Jessie was a nurse and had been posted to Launceston; she had not been able to travel down to the Huon since Sam had returned, although that would all change the following weekend. Sam intended to propose then.

I'll just be honest with them and see how I go, he decided.

Sam arrived at the building housing the offices of the Soldier Settlement Program and climbed the one flight of stairs. Introducing himself to the elderly woman behind the desk, Sam waited to be called in.

Fifteen long minutes later, a grey-haired gentleman opened the meeting room door and beckoned Sam in. There were four men on the committee; all of them quite old.

Sam was asked the questions; most of them were as he predicted, including the final question.

'Are you married Mr Wilson?'

Sam explained his situation, and to his surprise, the committee seemed quite satisfied with his answer.

'Well, Mr Wilson, I think we can comfortably say you meet the criteria we are looking for. Despite your lack of experience, the fact you grew up in the best apple-growing region in Australia puts you in good stead. Congratulations, we will confirm your acceptance by letter shortly.'

Sam thanked them all and departed, barely able to contain his excitement. He had arranged to meet his father at four, at the same intersection where he had been dropped off. The time now was three pm so he decided to take a stroll into Hobart proper; something the returned soldier hadn't done for a good four years. Arriving back at Argyle Street five minutes early, he found his father was already there parked opposite *The Mercury* newspaper building. Sam hopped in with a grin from ear to ear. His father looked at him with a wry smile.

'So, I take it you missed out then? The reason you're smiling is at the thought of becoming a policeman just like me.'

'Sorry, Dad, I'm going to be growing apples for the rest of my life.'

'Well, at least you'll still be in the valley, I take it?'

'I'm not sure. I'll be receiving a letter soon and that's when I'll know. I can't imagine it wouldn't be in the Huon… I mean apples are what we're famous for after all.'

Sam received a letter from the Soldier Settlement Board confirming his selection. The grant was for an existing apple orchard located in Grove in the Huon Valley.

The financial conditions were similar to Victoria's; 3.5% interest rising by 0.5% per year until reaching the commercial rate.

Sam was delighted; he would be farming in his home municipality; thus, close to his family and friends. Sam couldn't wait to tell his mother and father but most importantly, Jessie.

WHERE IN THE HELL IS EL ARISH?
CHAPTER 13

Albert finally arrived at the Townsville wharf, having stopped in Brisbane and Mackay along the way. His wife, Annie and his four-year-old boy, Levi, were there waiting to greet him. It was a wonderful experience kissing Annie and taking Levi in his arms for the first time. Annie's parents were also present and greeted Albert as a long lost son. They walked to where Jim, Annie's father, had parked his Buick. The family piled into the large automobile for the trip to Home Hill, about a ninety-minute drive.

Home Hill was located in the Burdekin District, the sugar cane capital of Australia. Jim and Emma owned one of the largest cane farms in the district; they were regarded as quite wealthy.

'Well, Albert you obviously kept your head down over there. It must have been pretty rough,' said Jim.

'Yeah, it was bloody rough, Jim... there were times when I thought I wouldn't make it back.'

'Have you thought about what you'd like to do now you're home?'

Blair Athol Homestead

Albert standing next to Annie seated, Jim and Emma to their right, Albert's brother John standing beside the car and his children are seated. John's wife, Anne is next to Emma.

'Yeah, I've thought about it. When we get home I'll talk to Annie about it and then we can decide.'

'Fair enough, you'd better keep the little woman on side. In your discussions, think about joining me on the farm, God knows we could use your help.'

'Thanks, Jim, I appreciate it; we'll consider that as one of the options.'

Annie gave Albert a look that indicated that option was the one she'd prefer.

They arrived at Home Hill. The name of the small town could have been derived from the family's homestead, a large rambling Queenslander, with verandas on three sides and raised off the ground by wooden posts. It stood on the very top of a hill overlooking the cane fields. They called the homestead *Blair Athol,* after Jim's ancestral home in Scotland.

The entire family, including Albert's brother John, his wife Anne and their two children, congregated in the lounge room for an afternoon tea of cakes and scones with jam and fresh cream.

'Well Bert, I bet it's been a while since you've seen a spread like this,' said John.

'Too right mate. I didn't think I'd ever eat jam again after eating the stuff with stale bickies for so long over there, but I have to admit this looks pretty damn good.'

After they had all eaten sufficient food, John and Albert went outside onto the veranda for a smoke.

'So, how was it really, mate? I've always regretted not being accepted to go.'

'I wouldn't worry. You were better off here. I don't really want to talk about what it was like. I'd prefer to try to erase those memories forever, although I doubt if I ever will. What I will say is that war is fucking horrible and any thoughts you may have had of adventure and excitement should be eliminated from your mind. The carnage, the despair, the horror of seeing your mates killed in the most disgusting ways are things you don't want to know about.'

'Hell, I'm sorry I asked. I promise I won't bring it up again.'

There was silence between the two brothers for a few minutes.

'What are you going to do now?' John asked.

'I haven't discussed it with Annie yet, obviously, but what I'd prefer is to take up the Government's offer of a cane farm somewhere around here. It seems the deal is a good one, and with bloody hard work, I think Annie and I could make a real go of it. I know I'd get plenty of useful advice from Jim and what with you being the manager at the mill I should do pretty well.'

'I don't know whether I can help you much. All the cane farms are on the same quota but you never know.'

Albert and Annie's Cottage

Albert began to settle into the Queensland way of life again. His wife had beautifully maintained the cottage they had built before Albert went away to war. It was located near the town of Hill End, and was not large but adequate for their needs.

Albert received a letter from the Queensland Soldier Resettlement Committee the week after returning from Europe. It requested his attendance at an interview in Townsville on the Wednesday of the following week.

Albert borrowed a suit and tie from his brother John; unfortunately; his foot size was much larger than his brother's so polished army boots would have to suffice.

John offered to drive him to Townsville and wait around to drive him back.

The interview went very well. The committee was very impressed that his father-in-law was the biggest cane grower in the district. His sobriety also impressed the committee; Albert lied, suggesting he abstained.

The young hopeful was informed that the committee would look very favourably when assessing his suitability for the scheme.

A letter arrived a fortnight later informing him of his success. A plot of one hundred acres of scrub suitable for cane growing had been allocated in a place called El Arish.

Albert thought this was a strange name for a region in Australia. It sounded more like a place you'd find pyramids and camels.

As it turned out, the town was named after a city in Egypt where the Australian Light Horse saw action in December 1916. The Queensland Government decided to name the soldier settlement area in honour of the Light Horse.

Now the letter was in hand; it was time to discuss it with Annie. Albert had to be at his best to convince her to leave their house and move away from her family for one hundred acres of scrub.

Albert suggested to Annie that they borrow John's car and go for a Sunday picnic on the coast. They arrived at Mission Beach about noon. Annie organised the hamper, and Albert laid out the rug.

They enjoyed their chicken legs and salad. Albert even brought along a bottle of Chianti purchased from one of the Italians that worked on Blair Athol.

After lunch, Albert broached the subject of becoming a settlement farmer.

'Annie, I've been giving a lot of thought about taking up the Government's offer to become an independent cane farmer. How would you feel about that?'

'Well, I'm surprised you'd even consider it; you know you would have a very good job working with Daddy at Blair Athol. We have a lovely cottage to live in, and our friends and family are close by; why on earth would you want to give all that up?'

'Annie, I've just had four years of taking orders, and some of them were outright stupid. I want to make it on my own; we can live or die by our own decisions. I know we can make it and become successful cane farmers.'

'Where would we have to go?'

'To a new settlement called El Arish. I know it sounds Arabic and it is. It was named after a place our diggers fought in during the war. It's not that far from here, about fifty miles.'

'Fifty miles is a long way if you don't own a car.'

'Don't worry, we'll be able to afford a car in no time.'

'Is it an existing cane farm?'

'No, it's pretty much scrub, one hundred acres in all, but it's been assessed by the Government experts as ideal for planting cane. I'll also grow other crops for us and sell the excess, and we'll need a paddock for livestock.'

'You've got it all worked out, haven't you, Bert?'

'Annie, I really want to give this a good go but if you're against it I'll drop it. It's your decision.'

'All right, I'll think about it, no promises.'

Annie talked to her mother and father about Albert's proposal at length.

Her father said, reasonably, 'Darling, it sounds as though Albert has his mind set on this, and you've got to remember the poor bastard has gone to hell and back. He probably mulled over the idea while in the trenches over there. It probably kept him going along with getting back to you and Levi. If for whatever reason the farm fails you know you've still got a home here, and Albert will have a job with me.'

'You're probably right, Dad. What are your thoughts, Mother?'

'I'm afraid I agree with your father, darling.'

'Well, it's not the end of the world, I suppose. I love Albert and want to support him, it's just... well, you know what I mean.'

'Go and tell him, darling, he'll be sweating on your decision,' suggested her father.

To Go Where no Other Sheep has Gone Before
Chapter 14

George received another letter from the Closer Settlement Board, informing him some documents needed to be signed. It also stated George was required to take possession by the 1st of May, 1920. An allocation of two hundred sheep had been granted and would be delivered to his farm at Mt Violet as soon as suitable fences and farm buildings had been erected.

A grant of two hundred pounds for fencing and building was allocated, and another fifteen pounds a month would be paid as a subsistence payment to purchase groceries and other essential items.

George composed a list of the materials required to construct the fences, including tools and timber, as well as material to build a cottage to house him, and his Border Collie whom he'd named Percy after his cobber who was killed at Pozières. The Board assigned him a consultant to assess his progress and advise George on sound farming practices. His name was Arthur Dobson, and he was an experienced farmer from Gippsland District in Victoria. Arthur reviewed the materials list and except for a few omissions like a kettle and pots and pans, he was happy with what George had selected to kick the farm off.

The last and most expensive investment was a large wagon and four Clydesdale horses to transport the load to Mt Violet in the Western Districts.

George set off on his long trek, leaving Melbourne on the 1st of April, 1920, and arriving at his plot on the 20th. The trip was difficult but without mishap, and the entire load arrived safely, albeit a little wet.

George Nearing Mt Violet

The fledgling farmer checked his map and confirmed the correct location for the lot.

'Yep, this is it all right, Percy.'

George got down off the cart and began to walk the land. Percy followed, sniffing the ground at every opportunity. It seemed a bit dry and the grass was sparse but still, experts who knew what they were doing selected it; George hoped they were right.

There was a large gum tree giving plenty of shade, so the novice farmer decided to move the horses under its canopy and give them some hay. He also filled a bucket with water that he'd brought with him. He filled a small bowl for his mate, who showed his appreciation with a lick.

Sitting down, George rolled himself a smoke. Looking out over the property, he concluded the right decision had been made. Although dry, it was beautiful land with many hills and mountains in the distance. George imagined his cottage surrounded by a white fence and sheep grazing in the paddocks. All in all, a good life was ahead. All that was needed now was a wife and a few kids.

Estates Acquired For Soldier Settlement 1918-30

1. Chocolyn
2. Chrome
3. Derinallum
4. Ettrick
5. Gala
6. Gringelona
7. Glenorchy
8. Hensley Park
9. Green Hills
10. Glenronald

11. Hilgay
12. Knebsworth
13. Koonongwootong S.
14. Koort Koort Nong
15. Korongah
16. Larra
17. Mt. Elephant
18. Mt. Violet
19. Murndal
20. Mt. Bute

21. Nangeela
22. Narrapumelap
23. Poligolet
24. Purrumbete S.
25. Struan
26. Tahara
27. Terrinallum
28. Wollaston
29. Woolongoon
30. Warrong

31. Shadwell Park
32. Kolora

18 Mt Violet- Volcanic Plains

The next day was the first day of establishing his farm; the first priority was to build sufficient fencing to hold the sheep.

George's life had changed for good, for better, or worse... time would tell.

The board had arranged for a farm hand to help George erect the fences. He arrived two days after George. His name was Harry, and he was a local who would prove invaluable to the novice farmer.

'Right Harry, we need to get these fences up as quick as we can, no fences, no sheep, no sheep, no money, no money, no food.'

'Fair enough, George, have you worked out where they're going?'

'Not really. I was hoping for your advice on that.'

'Well, how many sheep have they allocated to you?'

'They reckon four hundred tops.'

'Fair enough. Do you know how many sheep per acre they've estimated?'

'They reckon I should get three to four to the acre.'

'Mate, there's no fucking way you're going to get close to those numbers on this land. You're on the volcanic plains here so the water just runs off. I reckon two per acre at the most, maybe even one.'

'So you're saying we need to fence the whole two hundred acres?'

'Yep, that's what I'm saying.'

'Well, we'd better get started then. I hope we've got enough fencing to finish the job.'

The two men worked seven days a week, ten hours a day, finishing the last paddock just in time before Harry's time was up.

'I've got to thank you, Harry. I certainly couldn't have done it without your help, mate.'

'No worries, George. If hard work and sheer determination were all it took; you'd make a champion farmer. I just hope this block of dirt does the right thing by you.'

'Thanks, mate. She'll be right, I saved a bit of dosh while I was away so if I need to get more land, I will.'

'Okay, cobber, I'll drop by every now and again and see how you're doing.'

'Thanks, mate, I appreciate all the help you've given me over the past couple of weeks.'

'No need to thank me, George… the Government paid me.'

'I think you went far and beyond what they paid, Harry.'

'You take care of yourself mate; start building your cottage and finish it before winter. It gets fucking cold here.'

'I'll take your advice on that one.'

Harry mounted his fine chestnut mare and headed back to his home at Gala, twenty miles away.

George notified the Closer Settlement Board that the property was now fully fenced and ready to receive the sheep.

A letter was received back informing him that the sheep would be brought from a farm near Warrnambool and should arrive within a fortnight.

George had laid out stakes where he decided to locate his three-bedroom cottage; it was high on a hill overlooking the farm. The board was to organise the construction within one month of the fencing being completed, but building began three months later than the originally estimated start date. George had to resort to his small tent and swag for much longer than initially anticipated.

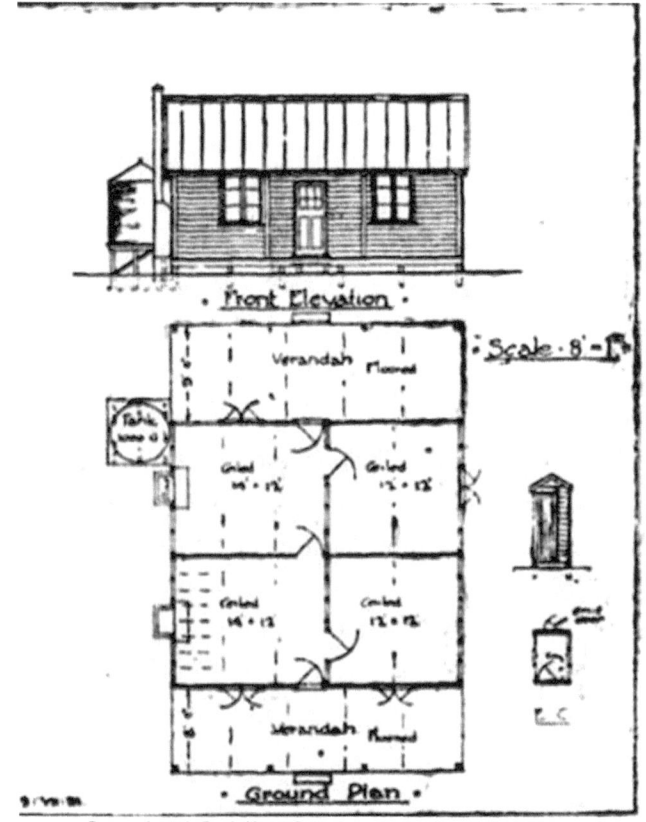

Standard Soldier Settlement Cottage Plan

The sheep arrived on time, and his days were taken up with installing water troughs and ensuring they had plenty to eat. The land didn't produce enough grass to feed the flock, so George was forced to truck in hay bales to supplement the poor pastures.

After a month on the land, the agricultural consultant employed by the board arrived for a two-day visit. The poor bugger had to put up with sleeping in the tent with George. His name was Evan Davies; he had farmed all his life and knew sheep inside out— literally.

George walked him around the farm and when they returned to the campsite, Evan had some bitter pills for George to swallow.

'George, you will have to work bloody hard to make a go of this property, mate. The quality of the pasture is poor... so poor you either have to invest in improving it or get rid of half your sheep. Having said that, the sheep you do have now will not sustain a living for you. The only way you can succeed is to increase the flock by at least another four hundred or preferably six hundred.'

'Well I don't get it. I get rid of half my fucking flock and that means I've got Buckley's of surviving. I increase the flock to one thousand, and I need another eight hundred acres. I just can't afford it, Evan.'

'I know it sounds impossible, but there is a way out. If you bring in superphosphate and improve the pasture, you can increase the size of the property in stages. I'll report back to the board and recommend they supply you with the fertiliser.'

True to his word Evan persuaded the board and a truck loaded with superphosphate bags arrived a month later. George spread the fertiliser from the back of the dray pulled by his beloved horses. It was hard and arduous work, but eventually, the whole two hundred acres was fertilised. All that was needed now was rain. For three weeks after George completed the land treatment the weather consisted of beautiful clear days with plenty of sunshine but no rain. Then, the skies opened up and didn't stop raining for a week. Eight inches of rain fell, the super soaked into the ground and three months later, George had good grazing pasture for his sheep.

What he still needed to increase was the size of his property; George learned that the adjoining block had not been taken up. He was able to negotiate the same terms negotiated for the initial block; i.e. 3.5% interest. This purchase increased his farm to just under five hundred acres. Having farmed the original allotment for twelve months, George was able to increase his yield to three sheep to the acre. In comparison with other soldier settlement farms, these were good figures; most farms didn't get more than one sheep per acre.

Most of the revenue earned from the wool clip was invested in superphosphate and farming equipment, including a tractor. This meant George could sell his four draught horses he but couldn't bring himself to do it.

George fertilised the new allotment immediately after getting the title. His aim was to purchase another four hundred sheep initially and he hoped the total flock of eight hundred head would increase organically through lambing to reach one thousand by the end of the second year.

Evan made periodic visits to inspect the progress George was making. The master farmer was impressed.

'George, you have been doing everything right, mate. You've listened to what I had to say about farm improvement and acted on it.'

'Thanks, mate, I figured you knew what you were talking about and I knew fuck all, so I'd better do as you suggested.'

'You've been here twelve months now. Have you had a chance to take a break from the farm?'

'Don't be silly. How could I get away?'

'I mean for a weekend. Why don't you come back to Warrnambool with me. You can stay at my place. You can even go to the Saturday night dance at the Palais. You never know… you might meet a pretty young filly.'

'Geez mate, I don't think I could go to a dance alone, not knowing anybody and all.'

'You'll be right. My daughter will take you along and introduce you to her friends.'

'Well, you know what? I could do with a little break. When were you thinking?'

'This weekend coming. You can hitch a ride with me.'

'And how do I get back?'

'That's a thought… maybe you'd better make it under your own steam.'

George's own steam was his brand-new bright red Massey Fergusson tractor; he estimated it would take him approximately three hours each way. George started his journey at six in the morning. Percy, as his passenger, kept him company. Except for a few fallen trees and very rough roads around Mt Violet, the travellers made it to Warrnambool by nine thirty.

Evan's farm was not far out of town, with lush green pastures and a view out over the ocean from the front paddocks, which was where the rambling homestead was located. George could only dream of owning such a farm.

After the farm inspection, Evan introduced George to his family, two sons, John and David and a daughter, Emma. His wife's name was Val; she looked like the typical farmer's wife; tall and strapping yet with a very pretty face.

It was obvious where Emma got her looks from as she was quite beautiful. George found himself looking at her then turning away in embarrassment when she met his gaze.

Val served up scones, jam and cream and prepared a large pot of tea.

Inevitably the kitchen table conversation swung around to George's experience in the war.

'How long were you in Europe for?' asked John.

'A little over four years, mate.'

'It must have been really exciting, I bet.'

'It was many things, John, but exciting wasn't one of them.'

'Did you see much action?'

'Yes mate, I did, more than I would have liked I can assure you.'

'Oh well, there might be another war soon and I can go.'

'I bloody hope not.'

With that conversation concluded, Evan suggested they take a trip into Warrnambool and discover the town's sites. What was really meant was, "let's go into town and go to the pub for a few beers."

The two men drove the ten kilometres into the coastal town and pulled up directly outside the magnificent building.

The two farmers, one of them experienced and one of them not, sat at the long bar and ordered two beers.

'Well George, what do you think of my spread?'

'It's great Evan; no doubt you've put some bloody hard yakka into it.'

'Yeah, I have, but it's been worth it, we make a good living out of it and the family is comfortable. You can have what I've got. You just keep working the place and keep improving it and you'll get there.'

'I hope you're right. Some days I wonder what in the fuck am I doing here. I still miss my family and being alone out there really means you're alone. I just wish I had someone to share it with, you know, the good times and the bad times.'

'Well mate, you never know, you might meet a sheila at the dance tonight.'

'In my dreams. I've got two left feet. I'll probably scare them away.'

'You'll be right, just ask Emma to give you a bit of a lesson before you go out on the floor. Don't worry about it. Most of the blokes around here can't dance for the life of them.'

The two friends headed back to the homestead for a lamb roast before Emma and George headed off to the Palais.

There was lots of laughter around the table and good country conversation. Emma checked her watch and indicated to George it was time to leave. Evan had lent them the Ford, which was fortunate, as Emma didn't fancy driving to town on George's tractor.

They arrived at the Palais and parked around the back. They could hear the music emanating from the building, and they walked in to be confronted with at least two hundred people dancing or talking in groups. George felt very intimidated. Emma sensed his trepidation and took his arm and approached a large group.

'Hello, everyone, I'd like you all to meet George. He's visiting for the weekend.'

Everyone in the group said hello and introduced themselves.

Emma led him over to one particular fellow named Andrew.

'George, Andrew served in the war also. I'm sure you'll have a lot to talk about, you know, swap war stories as they say.'

The two men smiled politely, but neither was keen to talk about the war other than the basics.

'So where did you serve, George?'

'The Western Front, mainly Flanders and France. How about you?'

'I started off in Gallipoli then Flanders. What Division?'

'The 1st. How about you?'

'The 2nd so we probably crossed paths.'

'Probably.'

Emma came over to the two returned soldiers and took George by the arm again.

'Come on, George. I'll teach you to dance; Dad said you were a bit nervous.'

'Actually Emma, I might wait a little while.'

'No, you won't. Now come on— it's easy when you know how.'

The pair walked into the middle of the dance floor where the band was playing *It's a Long Way to Tipperary*, a song George was very familiar with.

'Now, put your right arm around my waist, that's it. Place your left hand on my left shoulder. Good. You can come in a little closer, George, I won't bite you. Okay, just follow me, you start with your left foot as though you are stepping around me and I start with my right. George, we're turning just like professionals. Now, step forward two steps straight and I'll step back, good, now let's turn again. George, you're a natural.'

'I wouldn't say that, but I must admit I feel a lot more comfortable with you than with my previous attempts.'

The young couple danced most of the night and although George wouldn't give the Foxtrot a go, the waltz was much easier.

By the end of the evening, George knew he was infatuated with Emma and she was attracted to him.

They drove home to the Davies farm and, as they said goodnight, Emma gave George a kiss on the lips. It was not too passionate, but on the lips nevertheless.

George lay in his bed in the loft thinking about Emma and how besotted he was. He didn't know Emma found herself doing the same.

The family gathered next morning at the long kitchen table for breakfast.

'Well, George, how did you enjoy the dance?' asked Evan.

'I didn't think I would enjoy it but I had a cracker of a time.'

'Good; did you meet any pretty young ladies?'

George looked over at Emma and smiled.

'I'm afraid I monopolised George's time teaching him a few basic dance steps, Dad. There wasn't really an opportunity to meet anyone.'

'Oh well, now that you can get up on the floor you'll be able to ask a young lady to dance next time you're here, eh George?'

'Yes, that's right Evan... next time I visit.'

George prepared himself for the long and bumpy trip home. While saying his goodbyes to the family, he whispered to Emma that he would write soon. Sitting on the tractor for three hours seemed no time at all. His thoughts were with Emma and how to make an excuse to get back to visit her in the near future; the very near future.

The Closer Settlement Board were taking a keen interest in George's farm management. They were impressed with his land improvement program and the increased yield in his sheep per acre. They were keen to demonstrate how successful the Soldier Land Settlement Scheme was, not only to prospective soldier-farmers, but also to the State Government who was funding the program.

Another three hundred acres bordering on the top end of George's farm became available after the occupant walked off it in desperation. The board sent two members out to Mt Violet to talk to George about incorporating it into his property.

They found George clipping the arses of some sheep to ensure they didn't get fly blown.

'Hello, there. I take it you'd be George Harris?'

George looked up from his hunched position holding the sheep.

'I might be, but it depends on who's asking.'

'My name is Alfred Jones, and my colleague here is Frank Hall; we are members of the Closer Settlement Board. We'd like to have a chat when it's convenient.'

'Let me finish this one and we can go up to the cottage.'

The three men, two dressed in suits, and one in overalls, made their way to the cottage. They just spoke small talk along the way.

'Would you gentlemen fancy a cup of tea?'

'Yes thank you, George, that would be very nice.'

George poured the water into the old cast iron kettle and waited for it to boil. When the tea had been made the men sat at the wobbly kitchen table, perched on kerosene boxes.

'I'm sorry about the furniture. It hasn't been a priority until now.'

'Don't apologise, George, it's obvious where you spend your money and let's face it that's where it should be spent.'

The two men explained what had happened with his neighbour; George had no idea the poor man had forfeited.

'The board has decided to offer you the additional three hundred acres to be consolidated with your existing land, George.'

'Well, that's very generous but there's no way I can purchase more land at the moment. I'm right at my limit now.'

'No George, you misunderstand us, we are talking about gifting you the land.'

'What, you mean giving it to me… no charge no nothing?'

'That's right, the only condition we place on the deal is you purchase an additional three hundred sheep.'

'As I said, I'm right at my limit. I wouldn't be able to afford an extra three hundred.'

'We understand your situation, George. We would pay for the sheep, and you would only pay us back when the sheep have produced enough wool to cover the purchase.'

'Look, I appreciate what you're doing but I don't understand why. Where's the catch?'

'George, you stand out as a very successful soldier settlement farmer, and if the scheme is to succeed we need role models like you. The boys who are finding it tough can see, through your efforts, that it can also work for them.'

'Okay, I see your point.'

'Excellent.'

'It's a lot of extra work. As you know, I'm not afraid of that but it could also entail some extra expense. With the numbers I have now, using the communal shearing shed is fine, but with close to a thousand I'd need my own.'

'I see your point George. We don't have the authority to help you with a new shed but we'll take it back to the other board members and see what they say.'

'Okay, and I'll have a chat with Evan Davies and get his view.'

The three men parted company, and George went back to his sheep. He was excited about the prospect of increasing his land holding, but also excited about seeing Emma again.

Next day, George drove the tractor to the local store ten miles away. That's where the only telephone in the district was located. He rang Evan's number and Val answered.

George explained his conundrum and asked whether it was possible to visit the following weekend to discuss it with Evan. She immediately agreed.

To be honest, George was more excited about seeing Emma than increasing his farm size.

Returning to the property via the back paddock, George was concerned about a couple of the sheep and wanted to check them out.

'I'll have to practise my dance steps before I go back,' he said to Percy.

George started to pretend he was dancing the waltz with Emma, turning and such around the paddock. He was humming out aloud the Viennese waltz and unbeknownst to him, his neighbour and good friend Bill was watching him from the fence line.

'What the fuck do you think you're doing mate? Now, I know why your sheep always look so happy.'

'Oh shit, sorry mate, I'm going to a dance in Warrnambool so I thought I'd better scrub up on me dance steps so I don't make a complete fool of meself.'

'Thank God for that, I thought you had turned.'

They both had a good laugh and returned to the tasks at hand.

On Saturday morning at seven, George began his rough and ready trip to Warrnambool, arriving in time for morning tea. Val had baked some scones and the family and George sat around the kitchen table. There was only one person missing; Emma.

'Is Emma joining us?' George inquired.

'No mate, she's gone to Melbourne for a week visiting a girlfriend. She'll be sorry she missed you,' said Evan.

George felt his heart sink. 'Oh, I see. Never mind… maybe next time.'

Both Evan and Val could see the disappointment in George's eyes.

'George, you know you can come and visit anytime. I know Emma would love to see you,' said Val.

That took some of the disappointment away, knowing he could visit Emma without making up excuses to discuss farming matters with Evan made it easier.

Once morning tea concluded, Evan and George went outside for a walk. George told his mentor about the board's offer and asked for advice.

'Well mate it sounds like a bloody good deal to me, I'd jump at it if I were you.'

'Yeah, it does sound like an offer I can't refuse but I do have some reservations.'

'What are they?'

'I'll need my own shearing shed for one.'

'Yeah, you probably will. Did they say they'd help you?'

'They will discuss it with the board and get back to me.'

'What else?'

'I'm going to need a hell of a lot of super. The new property is worse than mine when I first arrived.'

'They helped you with that before; I reckon they'll front up again. From what you've told me they're doing this so they can put you up on a bloody pedestal and show you off to all and sundry. It's in their interests to help you as much as possible.'

'So you reckon I should go for it?'

'Fucking oath mate, you're on your way to being a very successful farmer with an income to match. Grab it with both hands.'

'The only other thing is labour. I'm flat out now looking after what I've got. How can I take on another three hundred acres?'

'Yeah mate, I see what you mean, you might have to hire a farm hand.'

'More fucking expense I can't afford.'

'George, it's up to you. If you take the risk and it works out you're laughing. If, for whatever reason, it doesn't work out, walk off the farm. Knowing you, I don't think that's going to happen.'

'Okay, I'll wait to see what the board will or won't do to help, then I'll make my decision.'

The following week, the two gentlemen from the Closer Settlement Board called on George again.

'George we have very good news, the board has decided to erect a shearing shed on your property large enough to cope with one thousand sheep. If you grow the flock over one thousand, the extensions would need to be borne by you.'

'That's great and what's happening with the super?'

'Yes, we have approved enough to thoroughly cover the entire property. Finally, we recognise the increase in your workload by taking on the additional land and sheep. We will subsidise a farm hand for the first two years. After that you should be able to cover his wages yourself.'

'Well gentlemen, I think we have a deal. I've got to thank you for the opportunity.'

'We obviously have a lot of faith in you George, so do your best.'

'Don't worry. I will.'

George was elated but also a little concerned by the weight riding on his shoulders. The board was relying on him to be a great success, something the farmer was also hoping for. If it came off, he might be able to ask Emma to marry him.

The first thing George did after the two board members left the farm was hop on his trusty tractor and drive to the shop and telephone Evan with the news and also to ask if a visit the next weekend was suitable.

Evan was elated and welcomed George to visit. This time the suitor asked if Emma would be home; she would be.

Saturday arrived and off George went on the Massey Fergusson, with Percy sitting at his feet, speeding towards Warrnambool at twenty miles per hour. Arriving just in time for morning tea, his heart missed a beat when he saw Emma's smiling face.

'George, would you like to take a walk down to the beach? It's beautiful down there.'

'I'd love to, Emma.'

They excused themselves from the table and headed towards the path to the beach. Evan and Val looked at each other and smiled.

'I reckon we could be looking at our future son-in-law, Val.'

'Let's not jump the gun, darling, but we could do a lot worse.'

The young couple walked side by side until they were out of sight of the homestead, then Emma took his hand and that's how they walked for the rest of the trip. Walking along the golden sand with the waves crashing onto the shore made for a very romantic scene. They sat down and George built up his courage to kiss Emma who responded with a passionate embrace. It was official; the young couple were boyfriend and girlfriend.

From that day on George would make the tractor trip with his mate to visit Emma every second weekend. Percy loved it too; the collie could play with the other farm dogs.

After another six months, George was able to purchase a Ford Model T pickup which made the trip more comfortable for him and Percy.

Finally, on the Christmas of 1923, having received approval from Evan, George asked for Emma's hand in marriage.

CANE FIELDS ARE BURNING
CHAPTER 15

24 January 1921

'I'm not going to Bagdad or wherever it is, Albert, if we have to camp out in the bush like natives. If I agree to go there, I want a house for Levi and me.'

'Don't worry, Annie. The Government will supply us with all the materials we need to build a nice little cottage. The place is called El Arish by the way.'

'How are you going to build our "lovely little cottage"?'

'Your father and John have offered to help me. Jim's bringing one of his farm labourers to help as well, and we all reckon we could knock it up in a couple of weeks.'

'Okay, here's the deal. You build the house and when it's all finished Levi and I will come up and move in.'

'That sounds fair enough. So you agree to come with me?'

'I don't really have a choice, do I? You're my husband and it's my duty to follow you wherever you go. Albert, I do love you and I can understand why you want to do this, but, you've got to understand my trepidation.'

'Of course I do, Annie, but I assure you this is going to be the right thing for all of us, believe me.'

Jim, the two brothers and Paul the farm hand packed all the material for the house, plus seed and fencing onto the back of Jim's truck. They also loaded tents and swags, food and cooking utensils. Their provisions were to last them four weeks.

They said goodbye to the family and headed off to El Arish. None of them had seen the property and were keen to assess its potential. They took four hours to reach the site with five creek crossings and roads that could only be described as rough. Finally, they arrived at Albert's block.

'When they said scrub they really meant fucking scrub, Bert. You've really got your work cut out for you, mate.'

'Nothing a good axe won't fix, Johno, she'll be right; all cane farms start off as a bit of rough ground don't they, Jim?'

'True enough Albert; ours wasn't that pretty when we started out. All right, let's unload the truck and set up camp, and we will start preparing the site first thing tomorrow,' said Jim.

The four men unloaded the truck within two hours; Albert built a campfire and lit it, ready to cook their evening meal. It reminded him of the days in Flanders when they were away from the front. That was the only time they ate well and on the odd occasion they'd steal a chicken from a local farmer and roast it over the fire.

This night they were having baked beans on toast, not quite the same as roast chicken.

They chatted around the campfire until ten and then retired to their tents. It was a beautiful starry night with a slight breeze; the perfect formula for a sound night's sleep.

The next morning they gathered around the fire that Albert had made and brewed a pot of coffee. There was one missing; Paul.

They sneaked up to his tent with a cold bucket of water and threw it over him. That woke him up.

'What the fuck is going on?'

'Wakey wakey, hands off snakey, mate. It's time you were up and about, we've got lots of work to be done,' said Jim, laughing.

Once all the excitement was over they all ate a healthy breakfast of toast and jam they then started the build. The first task was to choose a suitable site, and once the block was selected they cleared it of scrub. They dug the holes for the posts and took the levels with a length of hose filled with water. For three weeks, they laboured in the heat until at last they could stand back and admire their work.

Annie and Albert on the Veranda

Albert's agreement with Annie was to stay at the house and clear the scrub, then plant the cane, and when that task was completed she and Levi would come and join him.

Albert said goodbye to Jim, John, and Paul, and watched the truck disappear over the horizon.

'Right mate, you're on your own now. You'd better get on with it if you want to see Annie and Levi any time soon.'

Jim had promised Albert the truck if the scrub were cleared, and the cane planted within six months. The cane farmer knew it was a tough ask, but it was achievable.

Albert rose at 5am each day, seven days a week, and worked through to seven at night. The exhausted farmer would stumble into the cottage and cook up a rudimentary meal, have a cup of rum, wash up and go to bed.

At the end of a very hard and lonely six months, Albert had achieved his goal. He was delighted Annie and Levi would be joining him and the much needed truck would now be his.

Albert cleaned up the cottage so it was sparkling, or so he thought, and prepared himself for the trip to Blair Athol. Jim had agreed to pick him up and take him back.

Jim arrived in the truck, which Albert had decided to call "Old Bill" after the London buses used on the front to transport the diggers to the front.

Albert waited on the veranda, and soon saw a cloud of dust, heralding Jim and Old Bill.

'G'day Jim how's it going mate?' he said as his father-in-law got out of the truck.

'Pretty good Albert and you? I suppose you're looking forward for Annie and Levi getting here.'

'Yeah, bloody oath I am. Do you want to have a look at the crop before we go?'

'Yeah, I'd love to, mate.'

The two men walked the area where Albert had planted the cane first, some six months ago.

'It looks good, Albert. You should get a good crop in your first year all going well with the weather and all. Just one thing, I'd clear back the scrub from the cane field about another ten yards. You don't want that catching fire when you burn the cane.'

'Yeah, good point Jim, I'll get onto that when I get back here.'

'Right, let's go and pick up your family, mate.'

'That sounds good to me, Jim.'

The drive to Bair Athol was taken up with advice on how to increase yields and run livestock; the time went pretty fast and at last they were at the homestead. Jim pulled out the keys from the truck and handed them to Albert.

'Here you go, mate, you've well and truly earned these keys.'

'Thanks Jim, I really appreciate your generosity.'

'Don't mention it.'

Levi came running out to greet his dad, jumping up and wrapping his arms and legs around him.

'G'day young fella, how are you?'

'Good, I got a new scooter.'

'Did you now, you're a lucky fella aren't you. Who bought you that?'

'Gramps.'

'What a good bloke! Gramps gave me a new truck.'

'Did he?'

'Yep. Let's go inside so I can say hello to your mum.'

Father and son climbed the stairs to greet Annie waiting on the veranda Albert put his son down and gave Annie a huge hug and a kiss.

'It's good to see you Annie; I missed you.'

'I missed you too Albert, very much.'

Albert, Annie, and Levi entered the grand home to join Annie's parents for a Sunday roast lunch. It was the best meal Albert had eaten in months.

'When are you heading back to the farm, Albert?' asked Jim.

'I thought we'd try to get away tomorrow morning, Jim, there's still plenty of work to do as you can imagine.'

'I don't have to imagine Bert; I know what it's like.'

'Yeah, I suppose you do.'

'Where's young Levi going to school, Albert?' asked Emma, Annie's mother.

'They've just completed building a school right in El Arish so Levi won't have far to go when he starts next year, Emma.'

'That's good, now what about groceries and such how far to the nearest store?'

'They've built a general store as well and they've even built a church.'

El Arish Public School

El Arish General Store

'You'll have to come up and visit Emma; it's not too bad, is it Jim?'

'No, it's pretty good Bert; a few more years and it'll be a thriving town.'

'Did you know they're putting in a rail connection so the growers can get their cane to South Johnston refinery? In a year or two, the Tully refinery will be completed which will be larger and more advanced. So overall, the future for El Arish looks bright.'

Next morning, Albert, Annie, and Levi boarded Old Bill for the journey to their new home, saying their goodbyes to Jim and Emma.

The trip took three hours, and the family was all pretty exhausted by the time they pulled up outside *Memphis*. Albert had named the farm in keeping with the Egyptian theme of the area.

Annie looked at the rudimentary cottage, consoling herself to the fact that Albert had promised to extend it when the first harvest came in.

'Come on you two, come and see your new home.'

They alighted from Old Bill and entered the cottage. It wasn't as bad as Annie first imagined, and with a woman's touch it could be made to be liveable.

Albert showed Levi his bedroom, which was pretty basic, a single bed and a duchess.

The same décor applied for the main bedroom except for having a double bed.

The kitchen had a Kookaburra wood fired stove and very little bench space. These were things that could all be fixed, she thought.

Albert and Annie unloaded the truck, bringing in several chests. One was filled with her clothes and another with Levi's. The other two were filled with household items, including a new set of cooking pots and pans.

Annie insisted that they clean the cottage before unpacking everything. Albert thought this was a bit excessive, as he had cleaned the only the day before.

Eventually, the cottage was up to Annie's standards, the trunks had been unpacked and the cottage had taken on a completely new look. Pictures and photos had been hung on the walls and various ornaments decorated the shelves and the mantelpiece surrounding the cooker.

'Right, why don't you two boys go and inspect the property and leave me to cook dinner,' said Annie.

She gathered together some vegetables and placed a lamb roast she had brought with her in the oven. When Albert and Levi had returned the meal was almost ready.

For the first time in six months, the family ate together. Albert was feeling happy, as was Levi. Annie still wasn't sure that living in this remote location was the right thing to do.

The two boys washed and dried the dishes and cleaned the cooker while Annie went for a walk on what was a beautiful night. She was startled when she heard a loud groaning noise a sound she hadn't heard before. She quickly returned to the cottage.

'What's that horrible noise?'

'Don't worry, darling, it's just a male koala trying to impress a female,' said Albert.

'Well, it wouldn't attract me, that's for sure.'

'No, I suppose not… do you think I could?'

'You might be lucky.'

Annie put Levi to bed and made sure her son felt comfortable in the strange new room. His teddy bear was in the bed to keep him company.

Albert entered Levi's bedroom with a brand-new book called *The Boxcar Children*. Albert sat on the edge of the bed and read the first four chapters following the adventures of Henry, Jessie, Violet, and Benny. Albert was so engrossed in reading the story he hadn't noticed that Levi was fast asleep. Pulling up the covers, Albert kissed his son on the cheek.

'Is Levi asleep, darling?'

'Sound asleep, he's probably dreaming by now.'

'Well then, I think it must be time for us to go to bed.'

'That sounds like a good idea to me.'

They turned off the kerosene lamps and retired for the night. It had been six months since they shared a bed and their lovemaking reflected the long absence.

Next morning, the family shared a breakfast of boiled eggs from the farm's chooks and toast made from the loaf Annie baked the previous evening. After they had drunk their coffee and Levi had his milk, Albert left to work in the cane fields.

Annie busied herself cleaning the cottage further and baking a teacake to have as their dessert that night.

She asked Levi whether he would like to see what Dad was up to. The young boy gave her an enthusiastic yes.

They held hands and wandered down the rough track to the fields. The cane was now over six feet high and they couldn't see Albert at all. Annie called out but did not receive an answer.

Oh well, we could try walking through the cane, she thought.

They tried to push the cane away, but it was proving to be too thick.

'Come on Levi, I think we'll have to wait for Daddy to come home for lunch.'

Just then, the boy let out a scream and started to cry.

'Levi, what's wrong, darling? Did you hurt yourself?'

'Something bit me on the leg. It hurts… it really hurts.'

'Come on darling, let's get you home quickly and we can look at it.'

Annie picked up her son and carried him home to the cottage where she laid him down on his bed.

'Can you show me where it hurts, darling?'

'Just here, see.'

Annie examined the area on the leg where Levi had pointed. She went white, for there was two puncture marks a quarter of an inch apart. It was snakebite.

She quickly ran into the kitchen and grabbed a sharp knife and some bandage. She cut open the bite and attempted to suck the venom out. She then wrapped a bandage above the bite tightly to create a tourniquet.

She didn't know what else to do. Levi was very drowsy and when he attempted to speak, his speech was slurred.

Annie ran outside screaming for Albert who, despite being in the far field, heard her cries and came running. Albert ran into the cottage only to find Annie in tears and his beloved Levi in a near comatose state.

'What's happening?'

'Levi's been bitten by a snake.'

'Oh my God, it was probably a death adder; quick, we've got to get him to hospital.'

'Where?'

'In Tully, we can make it in an hour.'

The distressed parents lifted their son into the truck, and Albert drove as if a man possessed. Annie cradled him in her arms the whole way. She knew Levi was getting worse but couldn't do anything for him.

Finally, they arrived at the hospital where the boy was taken into the emergency ward immediately. The doctor injected antivenom into Levi's vein.

'We will know within the next few hours whether the antivenom has worked. Just stay with him and offer your comfort. He will know you're here although he's unconscious.'

Several hours went very slowly by but then, about 3am, Levi opened his eyes. Annie and Albert were ecstatic. Although unable to speak yet Levi looked at both of them and they knew their much loved son would be okay.

Albert raced down the ward looking for the doctor. He found him at the nurse's station, and both men returned to Levi's bed. The doctor examined the boy's eyes and took his pulse. He then used his stethoscope to listen to his chest, looked up, and smiled.

'He's going to be fine. We need to keep him here for a few days… maybe a week, then you can take your son home. He's a very lucky boy. Not many children of his size survive a death adder bite.'

'Thank you, doctor, we are so appreciative of what you did.'

'Well, you really should thank Albert Calmette; the doctor who discovered antivenom.'

'Where can we find him? We'd love to thank him,' said Albert.

'In France.'

'Bloody hell, I'm not going back there!'

After a week of convalescing Levi was allowed to go home, where he spent the next several weeks staying close to the cottage.

Albert was trying his hardest, working long hours, but he seemed to be fighting a losing battle. Apart from lower than average rainfall there was the dreaded cane beetle to contend with. His first year's harvest was approximately half what was initially expected, and therefore, Albert couldn't supply the refinery with the twenty acres of cane which was his allocated quota. Another year like 1924 and the farm would lose its quota, and then Albert would also lose the farm. The other obvious effect was that his revenue derived from the harvest was way down. Things in the Grimshaw house were looking rather grim.

Albert and Sammy Ploughing the Field

Albert walked in the front door after another frustrating day in the cane fields. The back paddock had just been planted, but there was the worry that the soil was too dry for the cane to grow. Exhausted, Albert slumped in the kitchen chair and asked Annie to pour him a glass of rum.

'Albert, we can hardly afford to eat let alone buy your rum.'

'Don't give me a hard time Annie, it's the only thing that keeps me going.'

'And what do you think keeps me going? It's certainly not stimulating conversation.'

'Just pass me the bloody bottle, woman, I'll pour my own fucking rum.'

'Don't you be going about swearing in front of the boy. You're supposed to set an example.'

'Fuck this, I'll drink me rum outside.'

Albert stormed outside, a bottle of rum in one hand and a cigarette in the other. The frustrated farmer walked down to the front paddock and lay down on the grass.

'This is not what it's meant to be like, fighting with my wife at night and working my arse off through the day for fuck all returns,' he said aloud.

'Surely there got to be something better.'

There wasn't; life continued on at *Memphis* with the same discontent for the next two years. The yield from the farm did improve, enabling Albert to meet his quota at the Tully refinery but Annie was miserable and if she was miserable, Levi and he were miserable.

Things came to a head on the 25th of November 1926, when Albert came home from the fields to find Jim and Emma in the cottage. Annie had two suitcases ready packed to leave.

'What in the hell is going on here?'

'I'm leaving you, Albert; Levi and I are going home to Blair Athol.'

'Bullshit you are, you're staying right here where you bloody belong.'

'Albert, don't make it harder than it already is, mate,' stressed Jim.

'You stay the hell out of it, Jim, it's none of your bloody business.'

'I don't care what you think, Albert. I'm leaving.'

With that, Jim helped Annie with the suitcases and loaded them in the car. Levi was bemused but had no option other than get in the car with his mum and grandparents.

'Goodbye Albert. If you stop drinking and become civil to me again maybe and only maybe we can get back together again. But not here. I'm never returning to this Godforsaken place again.'

The Plymouth drove off, leaving Albert alone. He walked into the cottage, took the bottle of rum off the shelf and dank himself into a stupor.

The next morning Albert staggered out into the fields and tried to work, despite his horrendous hangover. The dejected man just couldn't stop crying.

That night Albert came home to an empty house, no Annie cooking dinner, no Levi to talk to and joke with, just him.

Albert lived his lonely desperate life at Memphis for another six months with very little company other than Sammy his cattle dog and his neighbour, Jack Roberts, who would drop in once a week for a rum and a chat, comparing notes on the season and the cane market etc.

After a particularly heavy drinking session, Albert decided that enough was enough. His farm was failing and his marriage was gone, so what was there to live for.

Jack was inside his cottage, eating his evening meal with his wife and two children, when he heard a dog barking frantically. Leaving the table, Jack went outside to investigate; the dog was Sammy.

'Hey, what's up Sammy, what's the matter?'

Sammy just kept barking and began to run towards his master's property and when Jack didn't follow, the dog ran back and continued to bark even more loudly if that was possible. Sammy continued this routine until Jack realised what Sammy wanted. After letting his wife Lois know he was going to see what the fuss was all about, Jack faced the dog.

'Okay, Sammy, show me what you've found. Probably a snake or something so I better take my rifle.'

It took only fifteen minutes to reach Albert's place. Jack knocked on the door and entered. Albert wasn't there, so he walked around the back of the cottage.

Here, Jack found Albert with Sammy lying beside him. The poor bastard had shot himself; half his head was missing.

Apparently, Albert had taken his trusty 303 off the wall, the same rifle used right through the war, inserted a bullet in the breach, walked outside, sat on the ground, pointed the barrel under his chin and pulled the trigger.

He did what the Turks and the Germans failed to do; take this digger's life. *Lest We Forget*

SHE'LL BE APPLES
CHAPTER 16

Sam was waiting with great anticipation for the letter to arrive from the Soldiers Land Settlement Board; it had been two weeks and no sign of a letter in the mail. His routine was to check the mailbox about ten in the morning.

On this particular morning, Sam walked to the letterbox with the usual amount of anticipation and opened it up, only to see, on top of the other mail, the much anticipated letter. Ripping it open, Sam quickly scanned the text; in essence, he had been granted a twenty-acre orchard in Crabtree Road Grove. This was an area known for its premium apple growing.

The Tasmanian Government had purchased the orchard along with ten other twenty-acre lots from the Parsons family, one of the pioneers of apple growing in Tasmania.

The financial conditions were similar to Victoria's; 3.5% interest rising by 0.5% per year until reaching the commercial rate.

Sam was delighted; it meant farming in his home municipality, and thus being close to his family and friends. Sam couldn't wait to tell his mother and father, but most importantly, Jessie.

Silas Parsons, along with his wife and two young children, had decided to seek their fortune in New South Wales. They came out from England in 1835.

Their ship, the *Brothers,* arrived in Hobart Town on the 15th of November, 1835. Mrs Parsons suffered sea sickness for the entire journey and refused to board the ship again. Silas had no other option but to settle with his wife and two daughters Eliza and Roseanna in Hobart Town, where they stayed for the next four years. Silas made a journey to the Huon Valley to investigate its potential, and became excited about the fertility of the land. Having deciding to build a home near Blackfish Creek, he cleared the land of scrub and many large stringy bark gums over the first few years, and planted potatoes and wheat. After about four years, Silas planted the first apple trees.

He had to walk to Hobart every Saturday, leaving home before 4 am, bringing butter and other produce to where bartering would take place for essential groceries. Silas eventually procured a horse, which made the journey easier.

After a few years, the Parsons orchards thrived and became one of the major growers in Tasmania.

Silas Parsons

Sam decided to inspect the orchard, which was about six miles from Huonville, immediately. After saddling up his horse, Sultan, Sam set off on the ninety-minute ride. He checked the map and title of the property, which enabled him to locate the orchard without too much difficulty.

When the board described the lot as "established orchard", what they really meant was five acres of established trees, ten acres with very young trees nowhere near producing, and five of pasture. Sam knew he would have his work cut out for him just to survive the next few years with little income. The board had promised a living allowance, which he hoped would keep him in groceries and other essentials.

As part of the settlement program, materials for a house were provided along with a builder's labourer during the build.

Sam rode home and waited for his father to come back from patrol, at around four in the afternoon.

'G'day Dad, how was your day, mate?'

'Pretty good, no axe murders or drownings to report.'

'That's good. I received my official letter from the board today.'

'How did you go?'

'Good, I've been allocated an orchard in Grove, they subdivided one of the Parsons orchards into ten or eleven parcels.'

'So, how many acres have you got?'

'Twenty.'

'That's all right, are they good size trees?'

Sam explained the situation to his father together with his concerns.

'I'm a cop. I know very little about apples, son, but it sounds as though you'll be pushing it uphill to make a living. For the first few years anyway.'

'Yeah, I know, I've got to think of a way to generate an income. I thought about using the pasture to grow crops, but five acres won't be enough.'

'Well Sam, nobody's forcing you to take it up. You can always say thanks but no thanks and join the police force.'

'Yeah, I know, Dad. I think I need to decide what to do over the next week or so.'

The two men opened a bottle of beer, poured a couple of glasses and sat on the veranda looking out over the Huon River with the Sleeping Beauty Mountains in the distance.

'There's got to be worse places in the world than this,' joked Sam.

'Yeah, it's not too bad. Sam, have you had a look at where you're going to build your place?'

'If I decide to go ahead, and that's not certain at the moment, I spotted a hill on the area they classify as pasture. I'm not sure, but I think I'd have a pretty good view of the valley from there.'

'Well, Sam, you've got some serious thinking to do.'

'That I have. I think I'll ride out there tomorrow morning and spend some time there. That might help me decide.'

'Borrow the car; it'll only take you half an hour to get there.'

'Thanks Dad, I will.'

Sam headed off at eight in the morning and was sitting on top of the proposed house site by nine. The view was magnificent. He could see right down the valley looking left and Sleeping Beauty Mountain on the right.

Sam's House View

As Sam was looking over the orchard and contemplating how it was possible to eke out a living from the small orchard of fruit bearing trees, he had an epiphany. Rather than pick the apples for eating, why not brew apple cider and sell it through general stores and hotels? Immediately, Sam returned to the car and drove home to Huonville; there was some serious research to do.

On arriving back home, Sam immediately wrote a letter to the Soldier Settlement Board requesting a brewer instead of an orchardist as his consulting expert, and explained the reasons why. If the board agreed, his plan would go ahead.

The board answered his letter shortly after with an affirmative reply; Sam would become a brewer.

A truck arrived at the orchard carrying all the material needed to construct a cottage the following month. A local builder, John Green, also arrived to build the structure with Sam's help and his father's when time permitted. Two months and plenty of hard work later, Sam's cottage was complete.

Apple Trees for Cider

The next purchase would be a rudimentary apple press. Using this initially would determine how viable his plan was. An upgrade to a commercial quality press would be the next step.

Sam's First Apple Press

That weekend, Jessie and Sam would be reunited after four tumultuous years; Sam was becoming quite nervous.

What if she thinks I've changed? I've certainly aged. Four years fighting a war in horrible conditions would certainly age a man, Sam thought.

She was due to arrive that afternoon in Hobart by train. Sam had borrowed his father's motorcar to pick her up and drive her to the Huon.

The train was an hour late, which didn't help Sam's anxious demeanour, but at last the steam train pulled into Central Station. He could see Jessie, beautiful Jessie, leaning out the carriage window as the locomotive slowly came to a stop. She spotted Sam and waved frantically. Sam ran to the carriage and they held each other's hands, tears streaming down both their faces.

The conductor signalled that the passengers could alight from the train. Jessie hit the platform running and threw her arms around her man. They kissed passionately; it had been four years after all.

Sam collected Jessie's luggage and walked to the car; they didn't stop talking the whole way home. Sam described the orchard and his plans to brew cider, while Jessie described life in the Launceston hospital.

Sam had arranged dinner at the Huonville Hotel dining room; it was here where he planned to propose. He had purchased a diamond ring in Hobart. It wasn't large but nevertheless, it was a diamond.

Sam proposed after the main course, and Jessie had no hesitation in saying yes.

Jessie and Sam would be living in the small cottage in Grove. It was not luxurious, but adequate for their needs.

They were married three months later.

Sam decided to name his brew *Sam's Huon Valley Cider*, a very innovative name, which the cider brewer hoped would capture a reasonable slice of the market.

When the first apples from the five-acre plot were ready to pick, Sam elicited the help of his family and friends and they were able to pick most of the crop over two weeks.

Sam started to press the apples at night as his time during the day was taken up in maintaining the orchard and tending the market garden that had been established on the vacant five acres.

It was around this time that the long awaited expert brewer arrived to assist and consult. His name was Colin Woolley; he had worked for Cascade Brewery for over thirty years and was now retired.

'You must be Sam,' said Colin.

'I must be. And who pray tell are you?'

'My name is Colin Woolley, the Soldier Settlement Board assigned me to help you get established in your cider business.'

'Oh, I'm very pleased to meet you, Colin. My God, I surely need your help.'

'Well, we might as well get started. Why don't you show me your press.'

'Sure, it's over in the shed.'

The two men wandered over to a small corrugated iron shed and Colin peered inside.

'Where in the hell did you find this, Sam?'

'I bought off a neighbour for three quid.'

'I can tell you right now, mate, you won't be able to press enough apples in that contraption in a month of Sundays. That's made for the home brewer, not a commercial operation. How many acres do you have under full production?'

'Five with mature trees, and another ten that are three years old.'

'Okay, let's go and have a look at them.'

They walked down to the orchard and inspected the trees carefully.

'Sam, these trees are very healthy. I'd expect your yield to be between thirty and thirty-five tons. Is that what you picked?'

'Yeah, I reckon it was somewhere around there.'

'You mean you don't know?'

'Not really. We just picked them and threw them in the crates.'

'How many crates did you fill?'

'About one hundred and forty.'

'That's good; each crate holds a quarter of a ton so your yield would work out to be thirty-five tons. Spot on, mate— you've done well.

'The problem you have is those apples will rot in the crates before you can press them. We need to get you a commercial apple press, and we need to get it soon.'

'Colin, I just don't have the money to go out and buy another press.'

'I'll tell you what I can do, mate, I'll contact the board and explain your predicament. If they will lend you the money at low interest and pay for it out of the first two years' earnings from the cider, you should be apples as they say.'

'Do you think they'd come to the party?'

'All we can do is ask. I'll telephone Allan Hall tonight. If Allan agrees, the rest of the board will follow.'

Colin was true to his word, contacting his old friend Allan Hall, and after he explained the situation and gave Sam a bloody good reference, Allan agreed. It was in the interest of the board and the Government to have as many successful soldier farmers as they could.

Colin returned the next morning with a large commercial press in the back of his truck.

'Where in the hell did you find that, mate?'

'Let's just say I found it on the back of the truck this morning. Come on and help lift it off, it's a heavy bastard.'

The two men lifted the press off the truck and carried it over to the shed. It just fitted. It was decided that they should extend the shed soon but for now, it would suffice.

'Come on, Colin, where did you get it?'

'It was mine; I negotiated a reasonable price with old Bill and it was agreed we could install the thing today. The loan paperwork will take a couple of weeks, and we don't have that much time. We need to set her up and start crushing apples today. Have you organised the bottles and labels?'

'I think I've got enough bottles but I haven't organised the labels, yet.'

'Well, you better get your arse into gear, young man. You can't sell cider without a label on the bottle. I'll introduce to the bloke that does them for Cascade; all you need is a picture of an apple and the name.'

The two cider brewers drove into Hobart the following morning and met with Norm Cassidy; the printer that would produce the labels. They agreed on a design, and Norm promised them the labels would be ready for pick up in a week.

'Right, we need to get back to Grove and begin the crush,' said Colin.

They set up the apple press and began crushing that same afternoon; Colin estimated they should produce over forty thousand pints selling at twelve pence a pint; therefore, they should generate two thousand pounds, not an insignificant amount. In fact, that would amount to nearly four times the average wage in Tasmania. Sam had operating costs and distribution costs but even so, he estimated his net income would amount to twelve hundred pounds.

The pressing went well. The two brewers collected the apple juice in oak casks where natural wild yeast would ferment the juice. Colin decided after a month that the juice had fermented to the point where it needed to be transferred to barrels. Sam and Colin cleaned the oak casks so that any residue was removed, they then poured the juice back into the casks and stored them for another six months. Now, the cider was ready for bottling.

The next six months was taken up tending the vegetable crop and pruning the trees. Luckily, Jessie was earning money, albeit a nurse's wage, and the board paid Sam an allowance. It was tough, but they survived.

Finally, after six months, Colin gave the go ahead to bottle the cider. This was a laborious task, completed by hand with the aid of a tube and a funnel. It took three weeks to complete the bottling. Both Colin and Sam were more than happy with the finished product; Sam took a bottle up to the cottage where Jessie was resting. She had become pregnant and due to chronic morning sickness, had to leave her nursing job. That fact in itself made the successful marketing of the cider imperative.

'Jessie, have a sip and tell me what you think.'

'Sam, that tastes beautiful. I'd better not have too much or I'll get tipsy.'

'I reckon we're onto a winner here, Jess, we just have to get it out there so people can try it.'

'How are you going to do that, darling?'

'Colin will help me; we'll load up crates on his truck and we'll take it down to Huonville first, then Geeveston and Dover. After that we'll head south to Kingston and finally Hobart. Depending on how that goes, we'll head out to Glenorchy and New Norfolk.'

'That's a lot of travelling, Sam. Are you sure you'll be able to sell it all?'

'No, not at all, but we've got to give it a try, Jess.'

'I suppose you're right.'

The two entrepreneurs loaded up the truck with one hundred crates, each holding a dozen bottles of *Sam's Huon Valley Cider*, and headed into Huonville.

The first shop they tried was Lucy's General Store, where the proprietor, Lucy Baker, asked for a glass before she committed herself.

'That's really nice, Sam, I'm happy to order four crates.'

They were on their way.

They approached five outlets, including the pub, and four ordered quantities varying from one crate to the pub's order of six. They moved down to Geeveston and were able to sell eight more, and another eight were sold in Dover.

Sam was concerned about leaving Jessie alone for too long, so they decided to call it a day and head north the following day.

Sam waved Colin goodbye and headed up to the cottage where Jessie was lying down.

'Jess, how are you feeling, love?'

'Not very well, although better than I did an hour ago. How did you two go?'

'Really well, we sold forty crates.'

'That's great, where to tomorrow? Kingston?'

'Yeah and Hobart. That should be about it.'

'So you're going to do a bit each day?'

'Yeah, well, I don't want to leave you alone all day.'

'Don't be silly, darling, I'll be okay.'

'No argument, Jess, that's the way it's got to be.'

'I love you, Sam.'

'I love you too, Jess.'

Over the next two weeks Sam and Colin managed to sell all but ten crates of the cider. They decided they would hold on to those crates for personal consumption.

Colin's contract with the board to assist Sam came to an end, but the two men had become close friends and Colin would continue to call in to see how Sam and Jessie were going.

I'd Rather Have a Full Bottle in Front of Me
Than a Frontal Lobotomy
Chapter 17

Over the next five years Sam and Jessie's orchard hit full production but even so, Sam could not produce enough cider to keep up with demand. An approach was made to Bo Parsons to determine if Sam could purchase a twenty-acre orchard with mature trees next door. Bo and Sam agreed on a purchase price and after taking possession Sam had fifty acres of mature trees; twenty thousand trees in all.

Sam had progressively upgraded his equipment, and processing sheds to the point where the company now operated three electric apple presses and a mechanical bottling machine. His production was two and a half million pints a year. The company also sold one hundred and fifty thousand pounds of apples to other cider manufactures.

Life was good for Sam and Jessie. They had built a new house to raise their two children, John and Mary. They were earning a very good living from the apples, and the couple was respected throughout the community.

Sam and Jessie

Sam had built his work force to the point where there were four full-time employees and up to forty casuals employed for picking and crushing. The first person Sam employed was an old army mate, Dave Roberts. Although not one of the Invincibles, Dave was a good mate nonetheless. Dave became Sam's second in command and was irreplaceable around the orchard.

Dave was in the apple-pressing shed when he noticed one of the presses had jammed. This was not an unusual occurrence, as sometimes the pulp didn't get fully excreted and blocked the mechanism. The only way to rectify the problem was to crawl into the press and clear the blockage. This was quite a safe practice as the press tripped and had to be switched back on to restart.

Dave crawled into the press with a scraper and began to clear the blockage. Once cleared, he began to back out of the press. Something happened that had never happened before; the press restarted and came down on Dave with one hundred and forty tons of pressure. The poor man died instantly.

When Sam entered the shed looking for his mate, a horrific sight confronted him. Dave's legs were outside the press but the trunk of his body had been crushed to the point where there was only a three-inch gap between the pressing plates. Sam raced back to his office and called the police. His father had retired, but Sam still knew all the policemen stationed at Huonville. Frantically explaining to the policeman on duty what had happened, Sam pleaded for an officer to come to the orchard.. The police arrived thirty minutes later. The sergeant who had replaced his father was an old school friend, Steve McKenzie.

'G'day Sam, where's the victim?'

'In the pressing shed. It's not a pretty sight, mate.'

'Okay, let's go and take a look.'

'Do I need to be with you? I really don't want to see Dave again like that.'

'No mate, you can stay back; we'll take care of it. We'll need to ask you some questions later, so just make yourself available.'

The two police officers entered the shed and walked down to number three press.

'Oh my God!' exclaimed the junior officer, Ted Wilson.

'Shit, I've never seen anything like this before,' said Steve.

'Ted, we need to raise the pressing plate. You need to switch it on and see whether the plate rises, then we'll get him out.'

Ted did as instructed and sure enough, the plate rose immediately. Once at its full height, the machine switched off. If the two policemen thought what they first saw was horrific it was nothing compared to the sight that now confronted them.

They had never seen such injuries, not in all the car accidents they had attended or anything else for that matter.

Steve went back to Sam's office and found him sobbing with his head on the desk.

'Sam, I need to use your telephone to call an ambulance to take Dave away.'

Sam just uttered a guttural, okay, but didn't lift his head off the desk. The man was devastated.

The ambulance arrived soon after; they extricated Dave from the press and took him to the funeral home.

The funeral was held in the Huonville Anglican church, and attended by over three hundred mourners. It was a very sad event.

In the months after Dave's death, Sam became very lethargic and morose. The business was being affected as his decision-making ability had deteriorated to the point that the apple pick started three weeks late. This had a significant effect on the yield and the production of the year's cider output.

Jessie was beside herself; her husband wasn't sleeping well at night and seemed to be suffering from nightmares. Sam would become very restless and would scream out Dick's name.

Sam was dreaming the same nightmare every night; he was in the foxhole at Pozières with his cobber Dick, they heard a shell coming their way; Dick threw himself over Sam to protect his best mate from the shrapnel. Dick got hit in the head and back and died; his brain matter and blood covered Sam. That was how Sam was found an hour later shaking with fear. This was not a nightmare for Sam; this was reality, reliving what had happened to him in the war.

Sam could not shake off his despair and anxiety and he was suffering from severe depression.

Sunday 13th July 1927

The Wilson family had enjoyed a chicken roast dinner; the chicken had been killed and prepared by Sam that afternoon. After dinner, when the children had gone to bed, Sam excused himself from Jessie on the basis he was going for a walk and to smoke his favourite pipe. Sam walked down to the pressing shed and stood in front of the press where his good friend had died. Sam had refused to activate the press again after the accident; consequently, the cider brewery was operating with just two presses, limiting production.

Speaking to Dave, Sam asked for forgiveness. The returned soldier felt the same guilt for Dave's death as he did for Dick's.

Slowly Sam walked back to his office and took the 303 rifle that had been kept in a cupboard since the war. He loaded the magazine with four bullets. Returning to the house, Sam entered Mary's room. His beautiful five-year girl was sleeping peacefully. Her father took aim and shot her in the head, killing her instantly. Sam then calmly entered John's bedroom and shot him. Jessie, hearing the shots, raced out of the main bedroom only to find Sam with the rifle in his hand. Not saying a word Sam aimed the 303 and shot his wife through the heart. She slumped to the floor. Sam stood over her, crying, begging for forgiveness.

Sam walked outside, sat on the veranda squatter's chair and blew his own head off. What a tragedy.

Next morning, one of the permanent workers, John Oates, walked up to the house to get instructions for the day from Sam. Finding Sam on the veranda, Bill raced into the house, only to find the entire family massacred. The police were called and after a short investigation a murder suicide was declared.

Sam's Huon Valley Cider ceased to produce cider, and eventually the orchard, and the cider brewery, were sold to an investor from Hobart.

Almost everything comes from nothing.
Chapter 18

Mt Violet, Victoria 1926

George and Emma had been planning their wedding day for the past twelve months; now the day had finally arrived, Saturday 26 April. Emma had two bridesmaids; therefore, George had to rustle up a best man and a groomsman. The groom had written away to Albert and Sam, hoping they would be able to make the trip, but there had been no reply.

George chose his next-door neighbour and fellow soldier settler Bill Burgess as best man and Harry, the young fellow who helped him with the fencing, to be the groomsman.

George was able to purchase a suit in Warrnambool, the first and probably the last he would ever own. A white shirt and a black and white striped tie completed the outfit.

Emma's bridal gown was beautiful, a classic white wedding dress, and the bridesmaids wore purple.

The two scoundrels supporting George also bought suits they would probably never wear again, except for the odd funeral.

It was a beautiful day, and the ceremony was wonderful. Evan looked as proud as punch escorting his daughter down the aisle.

At the reception, Evan pulled George aside for a father-in-law/son-in-law chat.

'George, I'm a bit concerned that the little cottage you built on the farm will be a bit small for you both, especially when you decide to start a family. Val and I have decided to build you a four bedroom home on the property as our wedding gift to you both.'

'Oh come on, Evan, that'll cost a fortune! We can't let you do that; you're being too generous.'

'It's a done deal. The builder will be arriving on Monday and will be well started by the time you come back from your honeymoon.'

'What's it look like? Emma will want a say.'

'Don't worry, she pretty well designed the whole bloody thing. She's known about it for months.'

'Well, you're all a shifty bunch, aren't you? I was the only one not in on the secret. However, I can't thank you and Val enough, mate.'

The young married couple travelled to Melbourne where they boarded the *Duntroon* for a cruise up the Australian coast to Brisbane and back.

George and Emma's New Home

The new house took six months to complete. George assisted as much as possible, allowing for the time needed to be spent running the sheep property.

It was Christmas, 1926, when the newly married couple took possession of their new house. They called it *Passchendaele*, after the village in Flanders where George fought during the war. Most of the locals thought it was just a fancy French name.

George and Emma were getting excellent returns from their thousand sheep; wool prices were at the highest level for some time.

Despite having just moved into *Passchendaele*, they decided they should spend Christmas with Emma's family; they would then travel to Melbourne for New Year's Eve and see George's family.

Evan and Val asked to speak with George and Emma privately in the homestead's lounge room.

'As you are both aware, when Val and I die the farm will go to John. With him being the elder son, that has been the tradition in the Davies family since time immemorial. We have made provision for young David by purchasing another farm not far from here. We both believe Emma should have the same benefits as the boys; therefore, we are, with your agreement, willing to purchase another farm or farms to increase your property to two thousand acres. We also would purchase another one thousand sheep and help you with the land improvement expenses.'

'I don't know what to say, Mum and Dad, it's very generous of you although I hope it's a long way off. We want you two around for a while yet.'

'I think you may misunderstand, darling; we are talking about purchasing now when we are both alive and kicking as it were.'

'Oh my God, that's incredible! George, you're being very quiet... what do you think?'

'I am trying to comprehend it all, Em. I'm dumbfounded.'

George and Emma didn't have to think about it for long; they accepted graciously.

Fortuitously, two properties adjoining George and Emma's came on the market over the following six months. One had been abandoned by a soldier settler, while the other had been well cared for and would need little land improvement.

George now had two thousand acres to manage, running two thousand sheep; another farm hand was hired to help him; Harry his groomsman.

Emma had two children in two years, a boy named Gregory and a girl named Sarah. The wool prices were high, and they were exporting fifty per cent of their clip to England. George, Emma, and the kids visited Melbourne in September to attend the 1928 Royal Agricultural Show. Greg and Sarah loved sideshow alley and some of the milder rides, but George was there to look at a ram, and not just any ordinary ram; this beast was regarded as the best Marino ram in Australia if not the world. His ambition was to purchase it and, with careful breeding, produce the finest Marino wool in Victoria.

George waited in the auction pavilion for the ram to be brought into the ring, and, after a two-hour wait, the auctioneer brought out the magnificent specimen. The auctioneer started proceedings, inviting bidders to begin. There was a bid from the other side of the ring.

'1000 pounds'

'We have a bid of 1000 pounds, do I hear any more bids?'

'1500 pounds,' another bidder shouted.

'1500 pounds, do I have another bid?'

'2000 pounds.' A new bidder entered the fray.

George had not yet made his move, wanting to see the lie of the land before he made his first and final offer.

'2500 pounds.' The initial bidder was back.

'3200 pounds,' came a competing bid.

When the bidding rose to 4,000 pounds, George became nervous, as it was getting close to the amount they were willing to pay.

The auctioneer was attempting to coax another bid, but it didn't come. The hammer was raised. 'Going once.' There was absolute silence. 'Going twice.'

'4500 pounds.' George made his bid.

Everybody in the pavilion looked over at George in astonishment.

The auctioneer encouraged a competitive bid, but none was forthcoming.

'Going once, going twice, sold to number 356. Congratulations, sir, you have made a wonderful purchase.'

The other bidders and some very well to do sheep graziers wondered who this new upstart was. They would soon find out.

George went to the office and wrote the cheque, and the auction clerk informed him possession couldn't be taken until the cheque cleared. George was expecting that to be the case and arranged to extend the family's stay in Melbourne for another three days.

Once funds were cleared, the new owner carefully loaded the ram on the truck and drove it home. Emma and the kids returned by rail.

The breeding program was a success from the start, for the quality of the wool from the selected sheep was outstanding, achieving prices twice as high as what was paid before.

Things were looking very good for George and Emma, and they looked forward to an even rosier future together.

There was a popular saying… "Australia rides on the sheep's back". George and Emma were enjoying the ride.

Then, the world changed.

October 29 1929

Black Tuesday. The Wall Street Stock Market in New York, USA, crashed.

For Australia, the Great Depression caused commodity prices to fall, particularly wool, unemployment rose to the highest level in Australia's history and Australia's big cities were depopulated as thousands of unemployed men took to the countryside in search of agricultural work. At the same time, Australia had a lot of foreign debt resulting from infrastructure projects constructed during the 1920s. The lack of economic activity caused a massive reduction in the tax revenue collections. Australia was at risk of defaulting on its foreign debt. This prompted the Bank of England to send an envoy, Sir Otto Niemeyer, to Melbourne to persuade the Australian Government to slash government spending, cancel public works, cut public service salaries, and decrease welfare benefits. This became known as the "Melbourne Agreement."

The Unemployed Relied on Food Handouts

Passchendaele began to suffer, as the wool prices had dropped sixty per cent, hardly enough revenue being generated to pay the farm hand's wages and feed the family. George tended his vegetable patch, and lamb and rabbit were the meats they ate for the next four years. On the odd occasion George would shoot a wild pig, and the pork roast dinner became the highlight, as did bacon at breakfast.

There was a continuous stream of city folks knocking on their door looking for work. All George and Emma could offer them was a day's labour for a hamper of food. Generally, the offer was accepted. When shearing time came around there was never a shortage of shearers or tar boys, and they were always grateful for the work.

Many farmers didn't survive the Great Depression, but fortunately, George and Emma did. By 1939 things were getting back to normal. Then, the world changed again.

The Argus.

BRITAIN AND FRANCE AT WAR WITH GERMANY

CHAMBERLAIN'S DECLARATION

"OUR CONSCIENCE IS CLEAR"

AUSTRALIA PLEDGES FULL SUPPORT

LONDON, SUNDAY

'*Passchendaele Fleece*' had become known throughout the world as premium wool exported to the USA, Britain, France, and Germany to name a few.

One customer, Hugo Boss, boasted that *Passchendaele* wool was used exclusively in all his garments.

What George didn't know was that his wool was used by Hugo Boss to manufacture the uniforms of Hitler's SS troops.

George and Emma kept themselves informed from the Melbourne newspapers about what was taking place in Europe in the mid-thirties. George's experiences in the First World War made him extremely worried about Germany's aggression.

His concerns were well justified.

25th October 1936

Axis alliance concluded between Germany and Italy

25th November 1936

Anti-Comintern pact concluded between Germany and Japan.

Joachim von Ribbentrop negotiated an agreement between Germany and Japan that declared the hostility of the two countries to international communism. In case of an unprovoked attack by the Soviet Union against Germany or Japan, the two nations agreed to consult on what measures to take "to safeguard their common interests." It was also agreed that neither nation would make any political treaties with the Soviet Union. Germany also agreed to recognise the Japanese puppet regime in Manchuria.

December 1936

Law concerning the Hitler Youth made membership of the Hitler Youth compulsory for all boys.

14th March 1938

Anschluss (union) with Austria; annexing the smaller nation into a greater Germany. Hitler made a triumphant entry into Vienna

30th September 1938

Munich Agreement - was a settlement permitting Nazi Germany's annexation of Czechoslovakia's areas along the country's borders mainly inhabited by German speakers, for which a new territorial designation "Sudetenland" was coined. The agreement was negotiated at a conference held in Munich, Germany, among the major powers of Europe without the presence of Czechoslovakia.

November 1938

Kristallnacht (Night of Crystal)

The sounds of breaking glass shattered the air in cities throughout Germany while fires across the country devoured synagogues and Jewish institutions. By the end of the rampage, gangs of Nazi storm troopers had destroyed seven thousand Jewish businesses, set fire to more than nine hundred synagogues, killed ninety-one Jews and deported some thirty thousand Jewish men to concentration camps.

15th March 1939

Hitler invaded and occupied Czechoslovakia in contravention of the Munich Agreement. The Nazi war machine now controlled 66 per cent of Czechoslovakia's coal, 70 per cent of its iron and steel, and 70 per cent of its electrical power. Without those resources, the Czech nation was left vulnerable to complete German domination.

31st March 1939

Britain issued a statement guaranteeing Poland's independence. The issuing of this statement meant that if Germany invaded Poland, Britain would come to the aid of the Poles.

15th April 1939

Jack received orders to leave the American Embassy in Berlin and transfer to the embassy in London. He didn't need to be persuaded; things were getting well and truly out of hand in Germany.

Jack was allocated a two-bedroom suite at the Savoy, and an office in the U.S. Headquarters in Grosvenor House.

Berlin September 1939

The Germans concocted a story of Polish troops crossing their border and firing on various installations. In supposed retaliation, German tanks rolled across the Polish border during the early hours of September 1, 1939. Tensions were running high throughout Europe. Britain and France began mobilisation of their armies while Italy's Mussolini desperately tried to persuade Hitler to forestall war. The British and French representatives met with German Foreign Minister Ribbentrop warning that they would fulfil their obligation to Poland and go to war if German forces did not withdraw from Polish territory.

Paul Schmidt was a translator in the German Foreign Ministry and present at the history-making events of those last days of peace in Europe.

It is just after midnight on September 3, 1939, and the German juggernaut continues to slam its way into Poland. The Germans had not responded to an earlier British and French demand to withdraw their troops and a message is received stating that Sir Neville Henderson, the British Ambassador to Germany, wishes to meet with German Foreign Minister Ribbontrop. It is obvious to all that the Ambassador's message will probably mean war.

Ribbentrop decides that the translator Schmidt, should meet with the British Ambassador alone: the Minister was a bit busy.

It was after midnight when the British Embassy telephoned to say that Henderson had received instructions from London to transmit a communication from his Government at 9 am and that Henderson had asked to be received by Ribbentrop at the Foreign Office at that time. It was clear that this communication could contain nothing agreeable, and that it might possibly be a final ultimatum. Ribbentrop showed not the slightest inclination to receive the British Ambassador personally the next morning.

'Schmidt, you should receive the Ambassador in my place. Just ask the English whether that will suit them, and say that the Foreign Minister is not available at 9 o'clock.'

Schmidt's account:
> *The English agreed, and therefore I was instructed to receive Henderson next morning - that is, in five hours' time, it being now 4 o'clock in the morning.*
>
> *On Sunday, September 3rd, 1939, after the pressure of work over the last few days, I overslept, and had to take a taxi to the Foreign Office.*
>
> *I could just see Henderson entering the building as I drove across the Wilhelmsplatz. I used a side entrance and stood in Ribbentrop's office ready to receive Henderson punctually at 9 o'clock. Henderson was announced as the hour struck. He came in looking very serious, shook hands, but declined my invitation to be seated, remaining standing in the middle of the room.'*
>
> *'I regret that on the instructions of my Government I have to hand you an ultimatum for the German Government,' he said with deep emotion and then, with both of us still standing, he read out the British ultimatum.*

'More than twenty-four hours have elapsed since an immediate reply was requested to the warning of September 1st, and since then the attacks on Poland have been intensified. If His Majesty's Government has not received satisfactory assurances of the cessation of all aggressive action against Poland, and the withdrawal of German troops from that country by 11 o'clock British Summertime, from that time a state of war will exist between Great Britain and Germany.'

When he had finished reading, Henderson handed me the ultimatum and bade me goodbye, saying, 'I am sincerely sorry that I must hand such a document to you in particular, as you have always been most anxious to help.'

'I too expressed my regret, and added a few heartfelt words. I always had the highest regard for the British Ambassador.'

Ambassador Henderson Leaving the German Foreign Office

'I then took the ultimatum to the Chancellery, where everyone was anxiously awaiting me. Most of the members of the Cabinet and the leading men of the Party were collected in the room next to Hitler's office. There was something of a crush and I had difficulty in getting through to Hitler.

Hitler Seated at His Desk

When I entered the next room Hitler was sitting at his desk and Ribbentrop stood by the window. Both looked up expectantly as I came in. I stopped at some distance from Hitler's desk, and then slowly translated the British Government's ultimatum. When I finished, there was complete silence.

Hitler sat immobile, gazing before him. He was not at a loss, as was afterwards stated, nor did he rage as others allege. He sat completely silent and unmoving.

After an interval, which seemed an age, he turned to Ribbentrop, who had remained standing by the window.

'What now?' asked Hitler with a savage look, as though implying that his Foreign Minister had misled him about England's probable reaction.

Ribbentrop answered quietly, 'I assume that the French will hand in a similar ultimatum within the hour.'

As my duty was now performed, I withdrew. To those in the anteroom pressing round me I said, 'The English have just handed us an ultimatum. In two hours a state of war will exist between England and Germany.'

In the anteroom, too, this news was followed by complete silence.

Goering turned to me and said, 'If we lose this war, then God have mercy on us!'

Goebbels stood in a corner, downcast and self-absorbed. Everywhere in the room I saw looks of grave concern, even among the lesser Party people.

September 3 1939

Victoria, Australia.

Britain and France had declared war on Germany on the morning of the 3rd of September, 1939.

Just as the economy was starting to recover and *Passchendaele*'s prospects for healthier returns looked assured, the Second World War broke out.

George and Emma were naturally very concerned, not only for their livelihood but also for their beloved country. Australia had lost sixty-three thousand of their finest out of the four hundred and twenty thousand who had enlisted in the First World War.

Now, it was all happening again or was it just the continuation of the first one?

War can be good for the economy. Governments spend an enormous amount of money on weaponry, ships, planes etc., which helps the manufacturing sector. They also spend a significant amount on uniforms; uniforms are made from wool. George began to reap the benefits from the conflict.

As the war dragged on over the next four years, *Passchendaele* continued to prosper and George continued to invest in stud Marino rams and increase his flock.

Emma and George were grateful that their only son was way too young to enlist; Gregory was only eleven when war was declared.

Passchendaele's export market decreased; the farm was no longer exporting to Hugo Boss or any other garment manufacturer in Europe. It irked the two of them to know Hitler's thugs were wearing *Passchendaele* wool on their backs. They were however, still exporting to Britain and America and the overall volumes had not decreased greatly.

George was one of the few soldiers who had made a success of farming in Mt Violet, continuing to operate as a sheep grazier until his retirement in 1964 handing over the reins of *Passchendaele* to his only son Gregory, who had been working with his father since leaving Geelong Grammar.

The pedestal George was placed on by the land settlement authority was truly warranted.

THE GREAT EMU WAR
CHAPTER 19

Stan Nye had enlisted in the 11th Battalion, which was among the first infantry units raised for the AIF during the First World War. It was the first battalion recruited in Western Australia, and with the 9th, 10th, and 12th Battalions, it formed the 3rd Brigade.

Stan enlisted in Fremantle on 11 August 1914; passing the physical and being issued with his uniform and Enfield 303 rifle with bayonet. Stan was in the first group of recruits to begin training at the newly established training camp, Blackboy Hill, on the 17th of August.

This became Stan's home for the next ten weeks as the transition from civilian to soldier took place.

The 11th Battalion embarked from Fremantle aboard the transport ship *Ascanius* on the 2nd of November, 1914. Stan and the 11th arrived in Egypt to continue training in early December. After marching in the scorching heat with full pack and getting light relief from the pretty girls in Cairo, it was time to board a troop ship which would take them to Gallipoli. The 11th Battalion was not part of the initial landing; their turn came ten days later. A company from the 11th Battalion, including Stan, mounted the AIF's first raid of the war against Turkish positions at Gaba Tepe. Subsequently, the battalion was heavily involved with defending the front line of the Anzac beachhead. In August, it made preparatory attacks at the southern end of the Anzac position before the Battle of Lone Pine. The 11th Battalion continued to serve at Anzac Cove until the evacuation in December. Many of Stan's cobbers died on the Gallipoli Peninsular, but fortunately, Stan lived to fight another day.

After the retreat from Gallipoli, the 11th Battalion returned to Egypt. It was split to help form the 51st Battalion, and then brought up to strength with reinforcements. Stan was promoted to Corporal in the new Battalion.

In March 1916, the battalion sailed for France and the Western Front. From then until 1918, the battalion took part in bloody trench warfare. Its first major action in France was at Pozières in the Somme valley in July. After

Pozières, the battalion manned trenches near Ypres in Flanders before returning to the Somme valley for winter.

In 1917, the battalion took part in the brief advance that followed the German Army's retreat to the Hindenburg Line. The battalion subsequently returned to Belgium, to participate in the offensive that became known as the Third Battle of Ypres incorporating:

- Pilckem, 31 July to 2 August
- Langemarck, 16-18 August
- Menin Road, 20-25 September
- Polygon Wood, 26 September to 3 October
- Broodseinde, 4 October
- Poelcapelle, 9 October
- Passchendaele (First Battle), 12 October
- Passchendaele (Second Battle), 26 October to 10 November.

The battalion helped to stop the German spring offensive in March and April 1918, and later that year participated in the great Allied offensive launched east of Amiens on the 8th of August, 1918. This advance by British and empire troops was the greatest success in a single day on the Western Front, one that German General Erich Ludendorff described as "the blackest day of the German Army in this war."

The 11th Battalion continued operations until late September 1918. At 11 am on the 11th of November, 1918, the guns fell silent.

Stan sailed home to his beloved Freemantle in April 1919.

Having endured insufferable conditions in the trenches and a small piece of shrapnel in his leg, Stan had survived the war without serious injury.

On his return home, Stan decided to apply for a farming property under the Soldier Settlement Scheme. His interview went well; the returned soldier was accepted despite having no prior experience.

Stan was allocated a parcel of eight thousand acres of wheat growing land close to Campion, one hundred and fifty miles east of Perth. The land had been improved by the Department of Agriculture, and a small cottage had been erected.

The Cottage with Sally's Vegetable Garden

Stan was told that with hard work and diligence, he should be able to earn a good living.

Possession was taken in January 1920, and with the advice and help from a wheat-farming expert Stan sowed his first seed.

His harvest in 1921, being his first, was regarded as excellent, and this trend continued until 1932. Stan had met and married Sally, the daughter of one of his neighbours, and they had two children— both boys, David and John.

A full-time farm hand now used the original cottage and Stan and Sally had built a sizeable family home.

1932

Stan left the house at the normal time, 7am, to start his day working the farm but when he stepped onto the front veranda, the farmer looked out to the closest wheat field, and was horrified. The entire field was occupied by hundreds of emus munching away on the wheat that was due to be harvested the following week. Stan raced back in side and grabbed his trusty 303 rifle and began shooting towards the mob. They just looked at the furious farmer and kept grazing. It wasn't until Stan got to close range and actually felled a couple that the mob broke up and ran every which way, avoiding the bullets.

Stan jumped in his farm truck and drove out to inspect the entire property. In every field, emus were grazing. Knowing one man and a 303 was not going to make a skerrick of difference, Stan drove back to the house and telephoned all his nearest neighbours. Apparently, they all had the same problem. They all agreed to meet at the community centre that night to try and come up with a solution. If they couldn't find one they would all go broke.

There were over one hundred people gathered at the hall; obviously this was to be a very important meeting.

The farmer who was elected to chair the meeting was known to them all. Walter Stokes was not only a respected wheat farmer, but he was also the local Mayor.

'Okay, everybody, listen up. We obviously have a massive emu problem and somehow we need to resolve it. It's estimated there are twenty thousand of the buggers just in our district.'

'May I suggest a show of hands for those here who has an infestation of these bloody birds?' asked Frank Nelson.

'Good idea, Frank. Hands up everybody or should I say hands up all those affected.'

Most of the people in the hall raised their hands as Walter expected.

'Right, we know we've got a problem, a big problem, but how do we resolve it?'

'Do you think we could poison the crop?' suggested James Hall.

'I don't think so, James, if we poison the crop, we won't be able to sell any wheat for goodness knows how long,' said Walter.

'Based on all our experiences with the Department of Agriculture, I think asking them for assistance would be a bloody waste of time,' said Sam, a wheat and sheep farmer badly affected by the birds.

'Most of us are ex-military, so why don't we ask for the army to come in and eradicate the birds. Those they don't kill will scatter,' suggested Stan.

'Now that's a damn good idea, Stan. What does everybody think? Let's have a show of hands on that resolution,' said Walter.

Everybody in the hall showed his or her hands.

'Right, as Mayor I will make the approach and Stan, you, as the proposer, can support me.'

The meeting concluded with most feeling more positive than when they arrived.

Walter and Stan travelled to Perth where a meeting had been arranged with the Minister of War, Sir George Pearce. Stan and Walter had vivid memories of the effect of machine guns on the Turkish and German troops – so why not, they reasoned, use Lewis machine guns on the birds. The Minister agreed and ordered several Army companies to go out and save the crops. The Great Emu War had begun…

The problem was that from the beginning the emus proved to have considerably more acumen than their human opponents. Emus rarely formed into large groups, and when they did, it was difficult to predict where these big mobs would come together. There were some curious attempts to 'herd' the mob towards machine gun nests, but these involved small numbers, and relatively few were shot and even fewer killed. Reading the reports that survive, the Commander, Major Meredith, had a sense that the human combatants were extremely lucky not to lose some of their own to friendly fire…

The victor the spoils

The greatest battle of the campaign took place on the 4th of November. An Australian machine gunner, Corporal O'Halloran, had hidden a gun behind a dam wall and watched amazed as a thousand emus approached his position.

Waiting till they were upon him, the corporal gave the order to open fire. Twelve emus fell in quick succession and then the machine gun jammed…

A subsequent attempt to kill emus involved mounting a machine gun on the back of a lorry and driving it after a small group. Not a single bird was killed, not a single bullet was shot (the gunner had problems enough hanging on) and a stretch of fence was destroyed when the truck careered into it.

The campaign was ended by a series of mocking questions in the Australian Parliament on the 9th of November of the same year. When one wag asked whether there would be medals given for the campaign, a representative from Western Australia, A.E. Green, made the point that the medals should be given to the emus who had 'won every round so far'.

The most authoritative account of the war pays tribute to the emus themselves who are often sold as the recipients of human stupidity, but who were actually wily guerrillas.

'Each mob has its leader, always an enormous black-plumed bird standing fully six feet high who keeps watch while his fellow emus busy themselves with the wheat. At the first suspicious sign, the lead emu gives the signal, and dozens of heads stretch up out of the crop. A few birds will take fright, starting a headlong stampede for the scrub, the leader always remaining until his followers have reached safety.'

"EMU WAR" DEFENDED.

Justified by Damage Done.

CANBERRA, Friday. — The Minister for Defence (Sir George Pearce) in the Senate to-day warmly defended the employment of military forces and the use of machine-guns in the "emu war" in Western Australia.

Senator Guthrie (U.A.P., V.) asked whether it was possible to kill the emus by more humane, if less spectacular, methods.

Sir George Pearce replied that those who were not familiar with country in which emus were numerous could not realise the damage that the birds could do. Because of the drought in inland areas, the birds had come down in thousands to the settled areas. Through the gaps they made in the fences rabbits followed. Reports had made it appear that only a few birds had been killed by the machine-guns, and he had given instructions that operations should cease, but he had learned later that the birds had been killed in hundreds, and, as the result of renewed representations, the military party had returned. It was no more cruel to kill the birds with machine-guns that with rifles, and the wounded birds were despatched immediately the firing ceased.

The emus had won the day.

In spite of the problems encountered with the cull, the farmers of the region again requested military assistance in 1934, 1943 and 1948, only to be turned down by the Government. Instead, the bounty system that had been instigated in 1923 was continued, and this proved to be effective: 57,034 bounties were claimed over a six-month period in 1934.

Stan Nye and many of his fellow farmers continued on the land and became prosperous wheat and sheep farmers.

I'M NOT A LUMBERJACK AND THAT'S OK

CHAPTER 20

Frank, Joe and Philippe

Halfway around the world three Canadian soldiers (Canucks) were facing the same dilemma as their Australian digger cousins; what do I do now? The war had ended, and Joe Saunders, Frank Miller, and Philippe DuPont had fought for their country valiantly and had been shipped back to Canada to start a new life. The horrendous scenes they had witnessed, the German soldiers they had killed, the conditions in the trenches… these were all meant to be forgotten or at least placed in the back of their minds.

Two of the Canucks had decided to investigate the Government's Soldier Settlement Program. Philippe had decided to return to Montreal and continue his banking career.

The Canadian Government realised they were facing a major problem in reabsorbing discharged servicemen into civilian life. The Federal Government, working with the provincial governments, established a national policy for returned soldiers.

British Columbia was the first province to initiate a soldier settlement scheme.

It was this scheme for which Joe and Frank signed up. Frank had the support of his long time sweetheart and now fiancée, Sophie.

Both men lived on Vancouver Island in Victoria, a beautiful provincial city right on the ocean. The oldest city in western Canada, Victoria's origins lay in 1843 as a Hudson Bay Company trading post, named in honour of Queen Victoria. With the Fraser Valley gold rush in 1858, Victoria grew rapidly as the main port of entry to the Colonies of Vancouver Island and British Columbia. When the colonies combined, the city became the colonial capital and was established as the provincial capital when British Columbia joined the Canadian Confederation in 1871.

For most of the nineteenth century, Victoria remained the largest city in British Columbia and was the foremost in trade and commerce. However, with construction of the transcontinental railway, Vancouver, as its terminus, emerged as the major west coast port and the largest city in British Columbia.

Living so close, Frank and Joe could see each other regularly and discuss their progress with being chosen as a soldier settler.

'So Frank, have they given you a date for your interview with the Land Settlement Board?'

'Not yet. I keep checking the bloody post box twice a day despite only getting one delivery, just in case I missed seeing it the first time.'

'Geez mate, you're keen.'

'Joe, if I don't get selected I'll end up working in the mines like my old man. I don't want that. I've seen what it's done to him. Old before his fucking time.'

'Yeah, I know what you mean. That's about my only alternative, too. Either that or fruit picking.'

Another two weeks passed without hearing from the board. Then, on Monday morning, Frank checked his parents' letterbox and there it was, an envelope with the board's insignia. He ripped it open and quickly read its contents.

In essence it requested Frank to attend an interview the following Tuesday at the provincial government's offices to ascertain his suitability to enter the Soldiers Settlement Scheme. Frank raced back to the house and yelled out to his mother.

'Mum, it's arrived! I've got an interview next week.'

'Well done Frank. What are you going to wear?'

'That's a thought. I don't own a suit.'

'Why don't you ask Charles next door to borrow one of his. Working in insurance means a different suit every day, as far as I can see.'

'Good idea, Mum. We're about the same size. I'll ask him tonight.'

Charles was more than happy to lend the would-be farmer one of his suits as well as a white shirt, a conservative tie and a pair of black shoes. Frank looked splendid, looking like a young man going for an interview at a bank rather than with a view to becoming a farmer.

Frank went around to Joe's the following morning. Joe had also received a letter. Both pals were delighted but also nervous about the whole interviewing process. Over the next week they practised their answers to the possible questions; one asking, the other answering. By the time the interview came around, both Canucks felt quietly confident.

Frank was the first to be ushered into the boardroom, where six men sat at a large mahogany table. They went through the process of asking their questions including, 'Are you married, Mr Miller?'

Frank explained he was engaged and would be starting a new life as a newly married man.

The board members seemed impressed but did not indicate to Frank if his application had been successful. Frank would have to wait to receive their decision by mail.

Joe's interview was in the afternoon. He too answered their questions and had to admit his bachelorhood.

Both friends had to wait more than two weeks but at last they received their letters on the same day. They had both been successful and would be allocated farms on Vancouver Island.

Frank's farm was in a newly developed area called Merville, while Joe's was located in Creston.

The board had purchased land at Merville; it comprised fourteen thousand acres of deforested land formally owned by the Comox Logging Company. The development area was located in the Comox Valley on the east coast of Vancouver Island. The soldier settlement farms were about six miles from Courtenay, which was the business centre of the valley. There were good logging roads, plus the logging railway.

A board member, Mr M. H. Nelems, inspected the area before recommending its purchase, reporting back that the land had been extensively logged and burned, leaving it relatively clear with fifty per cent suitable for agriculture and the balance for pastoral purposes.

When a proper technical assessment was completed after the board's purchase, it was found that most of the soil was inadequate for farming.

Frank married Sophie on the 20th of September, 1920 and, after a brief honeymoon in Banff, prepared to take possession of the farm. A letter had been received from the board informing him the farm was fifty acres and the purchase price was $1759. They would grant him $500 for land improvement and $1350 for farm improvements. If desired, Frank could borrow a further $2500 for land improvement, erecting farm buildings and the purchase of stock.

The purchase price of the farm would be lent at the reduced rate of five per cent as would the land improvement loan.

Until the property had been inspected, Frank wasn't sure whether he would raise dairy cattle or turn the farm into an apple orchard. The decision was made not to avail himself of the $2500 at that point.

Frank packed his T Model Ford with his and Sophie's worldly possessions and headed off to a new life.

Joe received a similar letter although his lot was only twenty acres. The reasoning behind the small lots at Camp Lister, the name the board gave to the area, was that it was designated as orchard country and it was thought the settler farmers would have difficulty managing a larger plot.

The journey from Victoria to Merville took close to two days, over one hundred and fifty miles of dirt road. Frank and Sophie slept in the car, which was far from comfortable.

Frank checked the plot map the board had issued him and after some false starts, they found the land.

The description of the land the board had included in the information pack was "cleared land with good fertile soil suitable for dairy farming or sheep grazing." What was discovered was half the fifty acres had been cleared, and the other twenty-five acres was still covered in thick bush.

The cleared land was covered in logs, which would have to be sawn and removed.

'Well, Sophie, we've got our work cut out for us here.'

'We surely do, but look at the countryside, Frank. It's beautiful.'

'It's not so beautiful when we've got to clear it. I've brought an axe, but we'll have to buy a two-man bush saw.'

Frank and Sophie's Farm

They pitched their tent, which would be home until they built their cabin.

The board had promised the materials and a carpenter to help them construct it, but they weren't sure when either was due to arrive.

Both Frank and Sophie began sawing the logs, and stacking the wood for the fireplace they would one day have if the materials ever arrived.

Three weeks passed before a large truck pulled up on their block. At last the cottage materials were being delivered.

'Howdy, I've brought the building materials you ordered. Give me a hand and we'll stack it for you,' said the tall swarthy man.

'That's great. Did you happen to bring a carpenter with you?'

'Don't know nothing about a carpenter, pal. They just told me to bring this stuff out to you.'

The two men and Sophie laboured for two hours, finally emptying the truck of its burden.

The truck driver paid them his farewells and drove off, no doubt to pick up another soldier settler's building material.

There were some rudimentary plans that came with the materials. These were based on a Canadian Pacific Railway house.

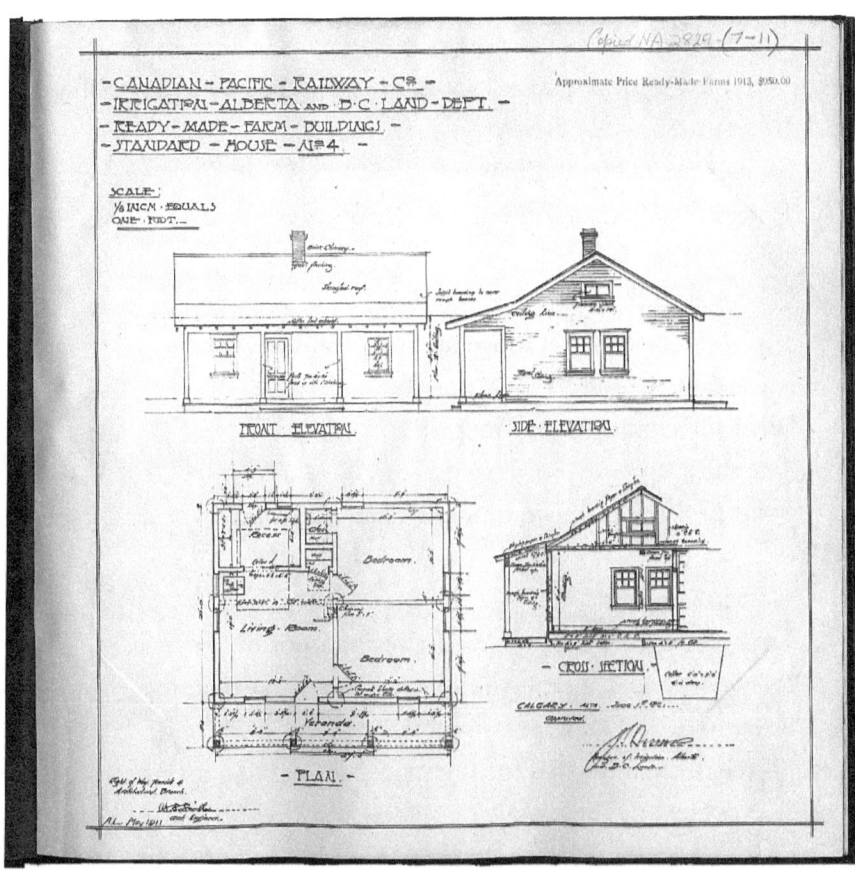

The building materials stayed where they were stacked for another month until, finally, Jack Rawlinson arrived on site and introduced himself.

'Howdy, the name's Jack and I've been sent here to build you two a house.'

'Welcome Jack; are we pleased to see you! It's been getting bloody cold in that tent and ogling that box that says "LOPI" wood cooker has been murder.'

'I take it you've picked your spot where you want to build?'

'Yep, we've got it all marked out according to the plan specifications.'

'Well come on, we better take a look at make sure it's not halfway down a cliff or anything,' Jack joked.

Frank and Sophie showed Jack the spot, and he detected no inherent problems.

'Okay, I suggest we start first thing in the morning. I'll pitch my tent close by; if I sleep in just rattle some pots and pans.'

The three ate a meal of sausages and mashed potato and sat talking around the fire for a while.

'So Jack, were you in the war?' asked Frank.

'I was in Flanders and France for about three years.'

'Yeah, so was I.'

'Where about?'

'Passchendaele, Vimy Ridge all over really.'

'Me too.'

'What division were you in, pal?

'The third.'

'I was in the fourth; we fought side by side under General Curie. Small world.'

'It was over there.'

'Let's change the subject. We're boring poor old Sophie.'

'Easy on the old, Frank you're five years older than me.'

'Sorry love; just an expression.'

The three of them retired for the night, hoping to get fine weather for the start of their project the next day.

Over the next month, the cottage took shape, and after six weeks it was completed, including the wood cooker installed in the kitchen.

Frank and Sophie decided they would establish a farm that would graze dairy cattle, poultry, and pigs with a one-acre lot fenced off for their vegetable garden. The plan was to grow enough for their own needs, and sell the balance at the market.

Frank wrote to the board requesting the $2,500 loan, which would enable them to purchase the stock and build and equip the dairy. The remainder would be spent on fencing and building a large chicken coop and piggery.

The cleared land had been cleaned up and fertilised ready for when the cows arrived. The next step was to clear the forested area. Frank contacted the Comox Logging Company and offered them the timber at no cost if they logged it and cleaned up the site when finished. They agreed and this set the precedent for many other farms in the Merville area.

After three months of logging, Frank and Sophie were the proud owners of fifty cleared acres.

They created a very productive little farm with the Comox Creamery taking most of their cream and their eggs.

The mining and logging camps in the area purchased most of the remaining produce. By 1922 Merville boasted a post office, school, church, general store, garage, community hall, and quaint tearooms.

Saint Mary's Church Merville

Merville became an active community with regular farmer's meetings as well as dances, concerts picnics, and in the winter, ice-skating.

Frank and Sophie became friends with a number of the other couples in the area, and Joe was a regular visitor to the farm they named *Hill View*.

Joe had also built his cabin on the orchard with the help of a carpenter provided by the board. He had planted 2,000 trees on ten acres, which were due to bear fruit after three years. The remaining ten acres was being used for dairy cattle although it hardly provided enough income to keep his head above water. Nevertheless, Joe persisted. Joe knew that when the orchard became productive he would earn a reasonable living. The novice farmer just had to keep going for a few more years. Joe also attended the dances, but there weren't any single women in Merville so he'd borrow Sophie or one of the other farmer's wives for a dance.

4ᵗʰ July 1922

The community got together for the 4ᵗʰ of July. Even though it wasn't Canada's national day, it was a good excuse for a party. American flags made out of butcher's paper by the school children were strung around the hall and red white and blue balloons were everywhere.

It was a great day; everybody really did feel that they were part of a very special community.

5ᵗʰ July 1922 Black Wednesday

Frank was working at the far end of the farm putting in some fencing. It was hot work; the summer had been an exceptionally hot and dry one. Smelling smoke, Frank looked up to the mountain; there was a huge plume of smoke billowing out of the forest. Frank raced back to the cottage. Sophie was lying down resting, she had become pregnant three months earlier and suffered morning sickness.

'Sophie, it looks like a forest fire on the mountain. There's plenty of smoke, so it could be a big one.'

'Are we going to be safe, Frank?'

'I think so. The wind would have to change to a southerly for it to threaten us but I'll keep an eye on it. How are you going babe, feeling okay?'

'I'm starting to feel a little better. I'll get up soon and do some work.'

'You just take it easy, girl, no need to push yourself; you've got precious cargo.'

Frank went back to his fencing, constantly keeping an eye on the forest fire. Around one in the afternoon, he decided to head back for lunch and check on Sophie. There didn't seem to be any major change in the ferocity of the fire or the direction it was taking.

Frank ate his lunch and chatted to his wife over a cup of tea. He looked at his watch and decided he'd better get back and finish the fencing. Frank walked out onto the veranda and froze.

'Oh my God, Sophie grab a few things and get out of the house. We've got to hightail it out of here right now.'

'What's happening Frank? You said it would be okay!'

'Obviously the winds turned; she'll be on us in five minutes.'

The fire swept through *Hill View* and every other farm in Merville. The village was also destroyed. By the end of the day, Merville was a scene of sheer devastation; not a single building had been spared, all the livestock and the orchards had gone, and all that remained was a landscape of black smouldering stumps and trees. The farmers' aspirations for a bright future had also gone up in smoke.

The fire destroyed fifty homes and pretty well all the farm buildings, wiping out the promising Merville settlement.

Frank and Sophie were left with the clothes on their backs, and a few possessions they were able to gather, including the Model T. The other settlers were in the same position and the only good thing to come out of the disaster was no lives were lost.

The Government commissioned a report by a "Committee of Reappraisal" with the understanding that any future policy regarding the Merville area would be based on the committee's recommendations.

When submitted, the report contended that half the land was worthless for cultivation and deemed useless. Mr F. R. Herchner. a committee member asserted:

> *"It will be a thousand years before the land at Merville will be fit to grow crops. The humus is absolutely destroyed. Some people, it is stated, have no choice but to go back to the land. This is very unfair, because even in the first place the settlement did not look a very promising place to make home."*

The recommendations to the Canadian Government were that the Government should reappraise the value of the land and grant title to each settler, taking back long-term loans, and withdraw completely from active supervision. The settlers were abandoned. These recommendations hastened the decline of the Merville area; many settlers sold up and moved back to

Victoria. Some stayed on their farms, but found work in the mines or logging camps. Frank was one of those settlers.

They rebuilt their home with the assistance of the Government and attempted to retain some normalcy in their lives. No sooner had they moved into their new home, than Sophie gave birth to their firstborn, a baby boy they called Neil.

Frank didn't enjoy working for the Comox Logging Company. Being out in the forests and enjoying the great outdoors was gratifying, but Frank just hated the fact that he was no longer his own boss, building a farming business for his family's future. Having gone through four years of taking orders, the returned soldier was back taking orders again. Frank never gave up the hope of returning to farming.

Sophie and Frank had two more children over the next four years; another boy, Adam, and a girl, Kate. Frank extended the house to include another bedroom, and the family was reasonably comfortable. The vegetable garden kept them in carrots, beans, and potatoes as well as various other vegetables, including spinach and kale.

Two milking cows supplied the family with dairy products, including cheese made by Sophie and later on, Kate.

Frank worked at the Comox Logging Company until retirement aged sixty-five; his last position was General Manager.

Joe had been spared the destruction of the fire; it was only the Merville area that had been destroyed. Joe tried to help his good friend Frank but there wasn't much that could be done other than help clear the rubble to allow the new house to be built and assist in building the vegetable garden.

Joe could no longer attend the regular dances at the Merville community hall, so he travelled to Courtenay. He had made friends with his next-door neighbour, Bill Clifford, a soldier who served with him in his battalion, though Joe didn't really know when on the front. Bill and Joe would head off to the dance at Courtenay on a Saturday night, hoping to meet the girls of their dreams. Generally, they would return disappointed but hopeful it would happen the next Saturday.

On one occasion, when Joe headed over to Bill's home to pick him up for the trip to Courtenay, Bill was waiting for him on his front veranda with a beautiful girl.

'Howdy Joe, we're all ready to go. This is my sister, Anna. Anna, this is my good pal Joe.'

Joe had fought in the Great War for four years, he had thrown hand grenades into German trenches and seen body parts fly. He had looked in the eyes of the enemy before bayoneting them and watched them fall, he had shot countless Germans in the heat of the battle… but nothing compared to the fear Joe now felt. What fear? The fear of making a fool of himself in front of the woman he had instantly fallen in love with.

She was beautiful, with long auburn hair, stunning blue eyes and a figure straight out of a magazine.

'Hello,' was all Joe could utter.

'Right then, let's get going, I promised Anna we would be there for the first dance. You might like to ask her, Joe, what do you reckon?'

'Yeah, sure.'

Joe just couldn't communicate. He was totally awestruck, and drove without saying a word while Bill and Anna chatted away.

Anna worked for the British Columbia Insurance Company in Victoria. Her job was to assess insurance claims for fire and flood; not very interesting, but it paid well.

Joe parked the car and the three of them entered the community hall. The band was playing Anna's favourite song, *Toot Toot Tootsie Goodbye*.

'Joe, do you dance the foxtrot?'

'Not very well, I'm afraid.'

'Come on. I love this song.'

'Go on, Joe, I'll have a drink waiting for you when you get back,' urged Bill.

'Well, I hope I don't step on your toes. As I said, the foxtrot isn't one of my best,' Joe said.

'You'll be fine; I promise I won't yelp if you do.'

They joined the dancing throng and Anna was pleasantly surprised to find out that Joe was a very good dancer. All that practice at Merville had paid off.

Foxtrots, waltzes and the Charleston took up the rest of the evening; Anna and Joe made a wonderful dancing couple. Bill also enjoyed the night, dancing with Miriam Davies, the girl he was sweet on.

During a waltz, Anna asked Joe, 'So what's the Joe Saunders story?'

'What do you mean?'

'Well, were you in the war with Bill?'

'Yeah.'

'In France?'

'France, Flanders and Gallipoli before that.'

'Bill won't tell me what it was like.'

'I'm sorry, Anna, but neither will I. You can't really explain what it was like, and I'm sure Bill's similar to me; he just wants to try to forget about it instead of talk about it.'

'I'm sorry, Joe.'

'Don't be sorry, I understand someone like yourself with a brother in the war and all would want a first-hand account.'

'All right, let's forget about that. What about now? What are you growing in your orchard?'

'Apples mainly, but also some pears and strawberries. I have a pretty big vegetable patch as well.'

'That sounds wonderful.'

'It sounds like a lot of hard work if you ask me. Now, that's enough about me… what about you, Anna?'

'Not much to tell really. I work in an insurance company, I live in Vancouver… Oh, and I love snow skiing.'

'I've never tried snow skiing. All I know about snow is it's bloody annoying when you're trying to fight in it.'

The dance drew to a close and the friends made their way home. Joe's initial shyness had long disappeared and the three of them chatted and laughed all the way home to Bill's property.

'Thank you for a wonderful evening, Anna, and Bill, I thoroughly enjoyed it. I hope I see you again, Anna. That was the best dancing I've ever experienced.'

'Thank you Joe, and yes, I enjoyed the dancing and your company.'

Bill and Joe continued to attend the Saturday night dances, but one month went by before Anna made another visit. Bill didn't tell Joe that Anna was staying with him so, when it came time for Joe to pick up his good friend, he got a surprise of his life.

'Anna, I didn't know you were coming! What a pleasant surprise. How are you?'

What he meant was, 'I haven't stopped thinking about you since we met. I think I love you and want to make babies with you.'

Joe composed himself and the three of them headed off to the dance.

Joe monopolised Anna's time, dancing and conversing, and it was soon obvious to Bill that both were smitten.

After a period of twelve months of courting, with Anna visiting or Joe catching the ferry to Vancouver, they decided to marry. It was also decided that Joe would attempt to either sell the farm or walk away from it.

Anna's salary was way higher than what Joe could earn from the still young orchard, and both of them were confident he would find work in or around Vancouver.

Fortunately, Joe's neighbour, Roy Smyth, purchased the orchard, which allowed Joe to pay back the Government loans and walk away with $150 in his pocket.

They got married in the spring of 1925 and honeymooned at Niagara Falls. Anna had a small apartment near Vancouver wharf and that is where they began married life.

Anna's father owned a building company, Vancouver Construction He offered Joe an apprenticeship, although he was past the normal age to begin such a career. Taking to it like a duck to water, Joe qualified as a carpenter in 1928. There was a building boom in Vancouver and the company flourished. Life was good for the young couple who now had two children, Amie and Joe Jnr and had moved into a bigger house that Joe and Anna's father had built for the family.

Bill's orchard had also done very well in those years; the orchardist now owned a property four times as large as the initial holding.

Then.

October 29, 1929 The Great Depression.

Canada was hit hard by the Great Depression.

The worldwide Great Depression started in the United States in late 1929 and quickly reached Canada. Between 1929 and 1939, the gross national product dropped forty per cent. Unemployment reached twenty-seven per cent at the depth of the Depression in 1933. Many businesses closed, as corporate profits of $398 million in 1929 turned into losses of $98 million as prices fell. Farmers on the prairies were especially hard hit by the collapse of the wheat price.

In late October, 1929, a mob of the unemployed raided a city relief office. On December the 18th, hundreds of unemployed marched through Vancouver's streets. The "snake march" became a popular way for demonstrators to tie up traffic and avoid police charges.

Jobless people from across Canada flocked to Vancouver for its warm climate and in hopes of finding work. The popular saying was that "Vancouver is the only place in Canada where you can starve to death before you freeze to death."

By December of 1930, long bread lines were common in the city, and hobo jungles and shantytowns started to spring up. By the summer of 1931, there were forty-two thousand jobless in British Columbia. In September of that year two hundred and thirty-seven relief camps were created outside the city, where men were forced to do roadwork. The men called them "slave camps."

Unemployed Working on the Roads

Vancouver Construction went bust in June 1930, throwing thirty men out of work, including Joe. The unemployed carpenter became one of the thousands lining up outside the Unemployment Relief Office every day.

Anna had two small children to care for so she couldn't work, which meant their mortgage payments were not being met. After twelve months, the bank foreclosed on their loan, and they joined the homeless. Fortunately, Anna's parents had enough room in their house to bring them in so at least they had shelter, unlike many other unfortunates.

Joe finally found work on the docks. It was hard work but at least it kept the family clothed and fed.

The family survived the Great Depression, although it took all their resilience to do so, and by 1938 Joe was back working as a carpenter, although not for Anna's father, Jim, who had retired a few years earlier.

In 1939 the world changed yet again, and Joe was able to keep working for the Second World War's duration.

Now, it was time for new soldier settlers to try their hand at farming, and Joe hoped the Government had learned from its previous experiences.

Frank and Joe entered the scheme full of hope and left it bitterly disappointed.

Would the same disappointment greet those soldiers who embarked on the final stage of the Great War –World War Two, twenty years later?

Here We Go Again
Chapter 21

John Healy's father, Ted, fought in the First World War, suffering shrapnel wounds to his right leg, which left him with a permanent limp. John was now about to embark on his own adventure, enlisting in the army at Victoria Barracks in Melbourne along with two great mates from school, Bruce Cook and Ken Jones. The date was the 20th of February, 1942, Singapore had just fallen to the Japanese onslaught and Australia was calling on its finest to help hold back the peril from Australian shores.

The three recruits were ordered to report to Victoria Barracks where they would be loaded on transports and taken to Puckapunyal. Here, they would begin their six-week training program. Because of the emergency in New Guinea with the Japanese heading for Port Moresby at breakneck speed, the training was reduced to two weeks. The boys hadn't even learned how to use their rifles, let alone care for them in the jungle conditions.

They were transported back to Melbourne where they were hastily loaded onto a troop ship, the *Duntroon,* and sailed off to Port Moresby to face the battle hardened and very experienced Japanese army.

'Well boys, it won't be long now before we start shooting up some Japs,' said John.

'Yeah, as long as I live through this seasickness, I can't wait to get off this fucking boat,' said Bruce.

'It's not a boat, mate, it's a ship,' Ken corrected.

'I don't care what it's fucking called. I want to get off the bastard.'

'You'll be right, mate; not long to go now.'

John was right, the *Duntroon* berthed at Port Moresby the following night. Once the ship was secured and the gangplanks lowered, the soldiers disembarked in an orderly fashion. What wasn't orderly or well-planned was the loading of the hold back in Melbourne. All the tents and food supplies were loaded first; therefore, they were the last items to be unloaded late the following day. The 39th Battalion was forced to sleep out in the open and had no rations to eat. Some officer had a lot to answer for.

Things were about to get worse; the 39th Battalion was heading for the Kokoda Track.

'Anzac created a nation; Kokoda saved a nation.'

His Excellency David Irvine, Australian High Commissioner to Papua New Guinea, 1998

The Fuzzy Wuzzy Angles

By the end of June 1942, the Japanese plan to isolate Australia from the United States was well advanced. Japan was establishing a major base at the port of Lae on the mainland coast of Australia's Territory of New Guinea. Japanese naval landing forces had occupied Buka, Bougainville and Shortland, which are the three northernmost islands of the Solomon Islands chain. Between May and July 1942, the Japanese progressively occupied more of the islands comprising the Solomon Islands chain. As each island was occupied, the Japanese built forward airstrips in pursuance of their plan to intercept military aid for Australia from the United States. By the middle of July 1942, Japan had occupied the southern island of Guadalcanal in the Solomons chain, and 2,000 Japanese troops and construction workers were engaged in building the airstrip, which would later be known as Henderson Field.

The next step in the Japanese plan to isolate Australia from the United States would be the capture of Port Moresby on the southern coast of Australia's Territory of Papua. Port Moresby was of vital importance to Japan. With the whole of the island of New Guinea and the Solomon Islands under Japanese control, Japan could establish naval bases and forward airfields on these territories from which it could strike deeply into the Australian mainland and intercept military support for Australia from the United States.

The Japanese had initially intended to capture Port Moresby in April 1942, but an American carrier-launched aircraft from USS Lexington and USS Yorktown on the 10th of March, 1942, and smashed the invasion fleet that the Japanese were assembling at Lae. The Japanese were forced to postpone the capture of Port Moresby until May 1942. When the Japanese finally launched a powerful seaborne invasion force towards Port Moresby in the first week of May 1942, their first attempt to capture Port Moresby was frustrated by a joint United States and Australian naval task force at the Battle of the Coral Sea. For the first time in the Pacific War, a Japanese invasion fleet was forced to withdraw, and Australia was saved from more intensive aerial bombardment and a grave threat to aid from the United States.

Despite these setbacks, the Japanese were still determined to capture Port Moresby. The Imperial Japanese Navy had operational responsibility for Japanese military operations in the South-West Pacific area, but with the loss of four of its six best aircraft carriers at Midway, and Shokaku badly damaged at the Battle of the Coral Sea, the Japanese Navy was no longer capable of mounting a seaborne invasion of Port Moresby. Faced with this dilemma, Japan's admirals decided to pass the task of capturing Port Moresby to the Japanese Army.

Japan's military strategists developed a plan for the capture of Port Moresby which involved a two prong attack. Tough jungle-trained troops of the Japanese South Seas Detachment, under the command of Major General Tomitaro Horii, would land near the villages of Gona and Buna on the northern coast of Papua, seize the airstrip at Kokoda, and cross the Owen Stanley Range by means of the Kokoda Track. Once they were over the mountains of the Owen Stanley Range, Port Moresby would lie open to attack and capture by the Japanese troops. The second prong of the attack would involve a landing by Japanese marines at Milne Bay on the eastern tip of Papua where Australians and Americans had been building a forward airbase since 28 June 1942. When captured, Milne Bay would provide Japan with an air and naval base from which Major General Horii's attack on Port Moresby could be supported by Japanese aircraft and seaborne invasion troops.

The task of crossing the Owen Stanley Range must have appeared deceptively simple to Japanese military planners studying maps in Tokyo. They had never seen this massive, rugged central mountain feature of the island of New Guinea, which separates the northern coast of Papua from the southern coast.

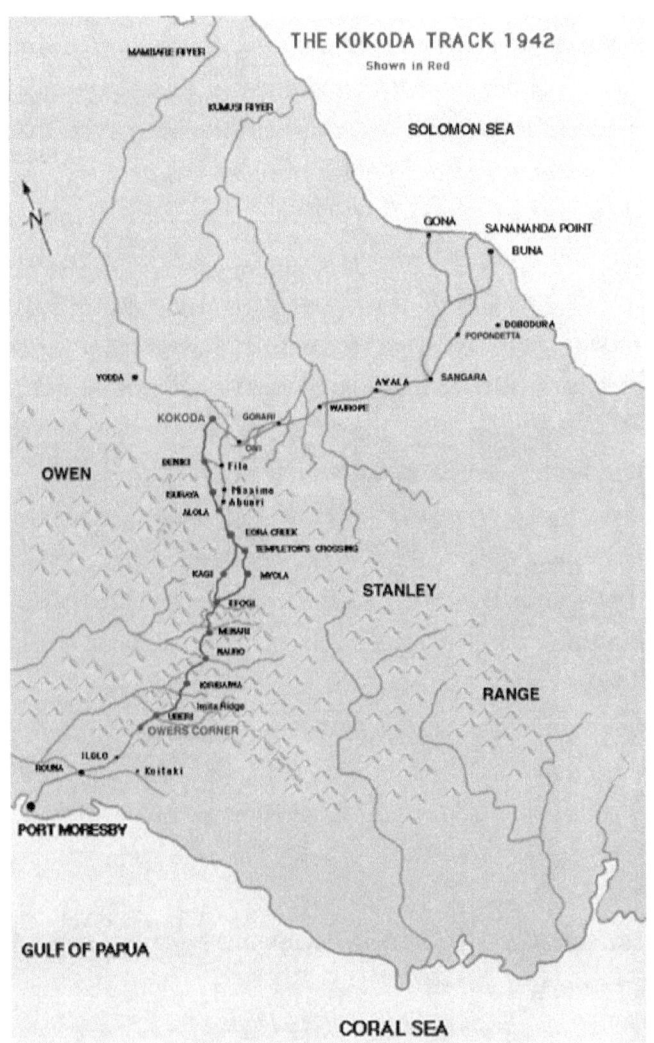

THE KOKODA TRACK 1942
Shown in Red

Battleground New Guinea

The dense tropical jungles and heavy rainfall of New Guinea provided harsh conditions for soldiers who fought there in the Pacific War. The first Australians to arrive in New Guinea faced elite Japanese troops of the South Seas Detachment on the Kokoda Track and crack Japanese marines of the Special Naval Landing Forces at Milne Bay. These tough Japanese troops had acquired extensive combat experience fighting in China, Malaya, the Philippines, and Dutch East Indies. They were experienced jungle fighters, and the dense jungles of New Guinea provided them with ideal conditions for their kind of fighting.

The Australians on the Kokoda Track were heavily outnumbered, ill-equipped, poorly supplied, inadequately trained for jungle warfare, and fighting a fiercely determined enemy. To add to their problems, conditions on the Kokoda Track were appalling. The narrow dirt track climbed steep, heavily timbered mountains, and then descended into deep valleys choked with dense rain forest. The steep gradients and the thick vegetation made movement difficult, exhausting, and at times dangerous. Razor-sharp kunai grass tore at their clothing and slashed their skin. In many parts of the island of New Guinea, including the areas where the Kokoda Campaign was fought, the average annual rainfall is about 5 metres (16 feet), and daily rainfalls of 25 centimetres (10 inches) are not uncommon. When these rains fell, dirt tracks quickly dissolved into calf-deep mud which exhausted the soldiers after they had struggled several hundred metres through it, and which bogged military vehicles to the axles. Sluggish streams in mountain ravines quickly became almost impassable torrents when the rains began to fall. Re-supply was a nightmare for the Australian commanders on the Kokoda Track, because every item of food, ammunition and equipment had to be manhandled along the track or dropped by air. Heat, oppressive humidity, mosquitos and leeches added to the discomfort of the rain-drenched Australian soldiers who were often without adequate food and even a cup of tea.

As if this was not enough for the Australian diggers to face, their other deadly enemy was disease. Malaria, dengue fever, scrub typhus, and dysentery flourished in these conditions and added to the misery of the exhausted Australians. Wet clothes and boots were a frequent source of unpleasant skin diseases.

Australian Militia Battalions are sent to guard Australia's northern approaches

In response to ominous signs in 1941 that Japan was preparing for military aggression in the South-West Pacific region, the Australian government undertook a rapid expansion of Australia's volunteer Citizen Military Forces, also known as the militia, for the defence of the Australian mainland and overseas territories. Although liable to be called up to defend Australia, these militia troops were inadequately trained, and lacked adequate equipment and weapons.

Between March and December 1941, the Australian Government moved three militia battalions to Port Moresby to defend this vital northern gateway to Australia. The average age of these militia recruits was eighteen and a half years. Unlike the second Australian Imperial Force (2nd AIF), which had been recruited to fight the Germans and Italians in Europe and North Africa, the military service of the militia soldiers was strictly limited to the defence of Australia and its island territories. To many in the 2nd AIF, who could not foresee Japan's entry into

186

World War II on the side of Germany and Italy in December 1941, the militia wore the uniforms of soldiers but without the risk of ever being involved in combat. This distinction between AIF and militia service led to the young militia recruits being branded "chocolate soldiers" or "chocos" by some AIF members. The scornful term "choco" was intended to convey a suggestion that the militia recruits would melt if exposed to the pressures of real combat. As if to underline their second-class status in the eyes of many senior AIF commanders, the militia recruits were denied adequate training and equipment, and treated with a cavalier disregard for their welfare and feelings. These attitudes produced ill feeling between the AIF and the militia, which Australia could simply not afford.

Although initially a volunteer citizen army, following the fall of Singapore on 15 February 1942, the Curtin Labor government ordered full mobilisation on 19 February 1942. Thereafter, all males aged 18-35, and all single males aged 35-45, became liable to conscription into the militia.

During the first half of 1942, the Commander of the 8th Military District, Major General Morris, had no experienced AIF troops under his command at Port Moresby. His main force was the 30th Australian Infantry Brigade, a militia formation comprising the 39th, 49th and 53rd Australian Infantry Battalions. With the exception of the 53rd Battalion, the militia were led by experienced AIF officers and NCOs, but the troops were almost all raw recruits.

The appalling treatment of these young militia recruits provides a damning indictment of Australia's Army leadership in 1941-42. None of these militia units had received proper military training before arriving at Port Moresby. The 49th Battalion reached Port Moresby in March 1941 without the most basic infantry equipment, and were immediately put to work as labourers - unloading ships, and constructing roads and buildings. The 39th and 53rd Battalions reached Port Moresby on the Aquitania in January 1942, and they could not immediately be fed and sheltered because their food supplies and camping equipment had been stowed at the bottom of the ship's hold. Many of the raw recruits of the 53rd Battalion had never handled a rifle until they were put on board the ship bound for Port Moresby. The 39th Battalion, which had been raised in Victoria in October 1941, was fortunate in that it had more experienced AIF officers than the other two militia battalions.

The important role played by Australian Militia troops in New Guinea

Despite their lack of adequate training, equipment and supplies, and despite the appalling conditions under which they fought in New Guinea, the heavily outnumbered militia soldiers of the 39th Australian Infantry Battalion would play a critical and heroic role in delaying the momentum of the Japanese advance along the Kokoda Track towards Port Moresby until seasoned AIF reinforcements could be brought into the battle.

Local units available to support the Australian Militia at Port Moresby

In addition to the Australian militia units, General Morris also had troops of the local Papuan Infantry Battalion (PIB) and the local New Guinea Volunteer Rifles (NGVR). The troops of the NGVR, all European and numbering about 450, were spread thinly across areas of the Australian Territory of New Guinea not occupied by the Japanese. The fortifications of Port Moresby in April 1942 comprised two ancient naval guns, a field artillery regiment, a heavy anti-aircraft battery, and a few mobile anti-aircraft guns.

Composition of an infantry battalion on the Kokoda Track in 1942

It is appropriate to mention at this point the composition of an infantry battalion, because references will be made from time to time to the components of a battalion when dealing with land battles on the island of New Guinea.

In 1942, an Australian Imperial Force (AIF) infantry battalion was composed of several companies, usually four rifle companies and a headquarters company, and designated respectively: A, B, C, D and HQ. Militia battalions often included a fifth machine gun company designated E. Each rifle company was composed of three platoons, which were identified by numbers starting from one. On the Kokoda Track, the number of troops in each of the components of an infantry battalion could vary significantly, and it is convenient to think in terms of a range of 450-550 soldiers when battalions are mentioned, about 100-110 for a rifle company, and about 30-35 for a rifle platoon.

The Australian Government recalls AIF Divisions to defend Australia

The surrender to the Japanese of Britain's so-called "impregnable fortress" of Singapore, and the seemingly inexorable advance of Japanese military forces across the South-West Pacific, caused the Australian Government in February 1942 to recall Australia's AIF 6th and 7th Divisions from the Middle East. When Singapore fell, Britain's Prime Minister Winston Churchill made it very clear to Australian Prime Minister John Curtin that Britain's highest priority was the defence of India, "The Jewel in the (British) Crown", and that no British soldiers would be provided for the defence of Australia against a Japanese invasion. As if to underline his apparent lack of concern for the fate of Australia, Churchill tried to divert the AIF troops to Burma when they were returning by sea to Australia. If the Australian AIF troops had been diverted to Burma they would almost certainly have been lost in another British Far East debacle, and Australia would have been under much greater threat from Japan. Although subjected to verbal bullying by Churchill, Prime Minister Curtin was resolute, and insisted that the Australian AIF troops be allowed to return and defend their own country from a threatened Japanese invasion.

On their return to Australia in March 1942, these seasoned AIF veterans were not sent to New Guinea to defend Port Moresby against a very real threat of Japanese attack, but were kept in Australia to defend the mainland against a possible Japanese invasion. The 7th Division was initially deployed on the coast just north of Brisbane to defend the so-called 'Brisbane Line'.

Hit the Track Jack
Chapter 22

The weather was atrocious, on that first morning, torrential rain, and the humidity was wavering around ninety per cent. The 39th's job was to help unload the ship, which they did with a cheery disposition, not.

Eventually, the hold had been cleared including their tents, and food supplies. Their commander, Captain Sam Templeton, ordered they take the remainder of the day off and cook up a hearty meal. The eggs and bacon with toast and tea were going to be the best tucker they would eat for a good while.

Captain Templeton checked the supplies of weapons and food rations and decided how much weight each of his charges would be required to carry on their backs.

Because of the remoteness of the track, supplies would be difficult to get through to the troops; therefore, each digger was required to carry very heavy packs and equipment. The minimum weight carried by each man was eighteen kilograms (about forty pounds), but with a .303 Lee Enfield rifle and other battalion equipment passed around in rotation; the burden for each man could reach as much as twenty-seven kilograms (about sixty pounds). Burdened with heavy packs, rifles, and ammunition, and wearing khaki uniforms more suited to desert warfare than a jungle killing ground like the Kokoda Track, Templeton and his troops set out on 7 July 1942 to climb the mountains between Moresby and Kokoda. They could not have realised at the time that they were marching into history, and establishing the initial foundations of Australia's Kokoda legend.

The three cobbers, John, Ken, and Bruce, were allocated their gear and ordered to join the battalion at the front of the Port Moresby Post Office which would be their starting point for the march into the mountains. Once all the diggers were loaded, the order was given by Captain Templeton to move off towards the far end of the town and head for the beginning of the infamous Kokoda Track.

'Jesus, mate it's hard enough on level ground carrying this bloody pack. God knows what it's going to be like climbing fucking mountains,' complained Ken.

'Don't worry, mate, we'll all get used to it, surely,' reassured John.

The 39th, inexperienced and filled with trepidation, marched along the Port Moresby dirt roads and beyond for a couple of hours.

They reached the beginning of the track at 5pm the following day, Captain Templeton decided they should camp there for the night and tackle the track in the morning. There was plenty of laughter around the campfires, and discussions on what might lie ahead. One thing they all agreed on was their enthusiasm to shoot some Japs and maybe even bayonet a couple. It was brave talk that would soon be tested.

Reveille was at 5am, breakfast of corned beef and biscuits was at 6.30am and at 7am they began their torturous trek.

As soon as they entered the track the jungle enveloped them. It was muddy from the continual rain, and the slope was severe so many soldiers lost their footing and had to be rescued by their mates.

John wrote a letter back to his father in Melbourne describing the conditions.

February 3, 1942

Dear Dad,

I've just arrived at a place called Kokoda. We've been marching in the most terrible conditions for the past ten days just to get to this little tinpot place. Apparently, General Blamey and his mate General Macarthur wanted it secured so the Japs don't get their grubby hands on the airfield.

We started out on what they call the Kokoda Track two days after we berthed at Port Moresby. As soon as you hit the track, the jungle engulfs you. The first section was downhill all the way and I mean downhill, it's a seven hundred and forty odd metres decline. This place never stops raining so the track is just mud and you slip and slide all the way down. A couple of blokes hurt themselves pretty bad and had to be stretchered by the fuzzy wuzzies. That's what the local natives are called by all of us. Good blokes and great workers.

It took us the best part of a day to get down this monster. We camped at the bottom of a ridge called Imita. I've got no idea what that means. We made shelters out of bits of the jungle... you know, palm fronds and tree branches etc. Didn't help much. The insects were unrelenting the little bastards. I got bitten all over as did everybody else. Next morning, after a delightful breakfast of corned beef, biscuits and tea, we headed out to climb the other side, all eight hundred and fifty metres of it. Carrying the pack they've given us up a ridge like that is no easy task, I can tell you. We had to rest for five minutes after every hundred metres climbed.

Your legs ache, your back aches and you're soaking wet. The ridge was only about twenty metres wide so we had to descend to a plateau about three hundred metres where we camped for the night. By the time I reached the campsite my legs were wobbly. They call it laughing knees. Well, as far as I'm concerned, it was no laughing matter I could hardly walk.

We just got settled for the night when a bloody big storm hit us I've never seen rain or lightning like it and the thunder must have sounded like the big guns you had to endure in your time.

Our tents were soaked so we slept in puddles for the remainder of the night.

We haven't sighted any Japs yet. Mind you, that's not to say they're not out there watching every move we make and just waiting for the right opportunity.

What's frustrating is you walk eight or ten miles in a day and arrive at the next camp totally exhausted and realise you've only actually covered two miles in actual distance. Most of it has been up and down.

The next camp was a native grass hut it had no walls so the rain just pissed in, and everybody gets soaked. It was bitterly cold, because our elevation was about four thousand feet. So there I was wet, cold, and in a native hut with little shelter. What else could go wrong?

Native rats biting my hair and scratching my nose and insects eating me alive, that's what.

The next week was just more of the same climbing and descending, climbing and descending. The pack seems to be getting heavier and heavier, and my uniform hasn't been dry since I left Moresby.

At last, we made it to Kokoda safe and sound, but the fighting will start any minute. I'll keep my head down as you advised me to do before I left for this place.

Love to Mum and Jessie.

Your son

John

Taking a Well-Earned Rest

AGAINST ALL THE ODDS
CHAPTER 23

23 July 1942

Captain Templeton assessed the chances of his men holding back a Japanese attack on the lightly defended airfield, and he wasn't confident. His intelligence informed him that two thousand Japanese troops had landed at Gona and were heading their way. Templeton took the decision to send 11 Platoon back to the Wairopi River with orders to retreat further back to Gorari if they encountered Japanese troops.

'Hey Johno, what's with fall back if we see any Japs? I thought we were here to beat the shit out of the bastards, not scamper back to safety with our tails between our legs if we see one of the little yellow pricks,' said Ken.

'Yeah, I know what you're talking about, mate. It seems bloody stupid to me,' answered John.

'Shut up you two. I think I just saw some Japs over the other side of the river,' whispered Bruce.

'Bruce, crawl over to Templeton, and let him know,' whispered John.

Bruce kept low, trying not to make any noise as he crawled through the jungle foliage. He found Captain Templeton with field glasses up to his eyes, scouring the river and the bush beyond.

'Sir, we have spotted some Japs coming up to the river, any instructions?'

'Continue to stay low and don't fire unless fired upon. We have no idea how many of them there are. My guess is these Japs are the forward party for the group that landed at Gona. If that's the case they'll have plenty of back up if we engage them now.'

At that moment, the two Australians heard gunfire.

'Damn it, they've spotted us. Return their fire, then we need to get the hell out of here.'

John Healy Firing on the Japanese

The platoon, along with Major Watson's Papa troops, withdrew to Gorari to join the 12 Platoon. The Australians suffered no casualties, while five Japanese were shot dead.

24 July 1942

Captain Templeton and Lieutenant-Colonel Owen along with their troops arrived in Gorari early on the morning of 24 July to join up with 11 and 12 Platoons.

The two officers were expecting reinforcements at Kokoda, so they decided to try and slow the Japanese advance by setting up an ambush on the track leading from the Kumusi River to Gorari. They and the remaining men then returned to Kokoda to welcome the reinforcements coming in from Port Moresby.

The ambush didn't delay the Japanese advance for long, and five hundred jungle warfare veterans of the Japanese 144th Regiment continued on in pursuit of the two Australian Platoons.

The Australians fought a valiant rear-guard withdrawal down the track to the village of Oivi where they intended to make a stand.

Lieutenant-Colonel Owen knew C Company of his battalion was on the track heading for Kokoda, but these troops were six days away. Owen feared for the airstrip with the Japanese advancing so rapidly. Upon radioing Port

Moresby that night, 25 July; Owen informed Major General Morris of the dire situation and requested two of his rifle companies be flown into Kokoda the following morning; a twenty-minute flight.

26 July 1942

Aircraft landed at Kokoda with one platoon of D Company of the 39th Battalion in two separate flights. All in all, fifteen men arrived and were immediately deployed to reinforce the two platoons at Oivi. Morris did not dispatch any more reinforcements to Kokoda.

That morning, the Japanese aggressively attacked the beleaguered Australians, giving the boys a taste of Japanese jungle fighting; a taste that would be with them for the remainder of the campaign.

The Japanese came in waves with no regard for their own lives. They were expendable, as Emperor Hirohito owned the life of every soldier.

'Fucking hell, mate! I reckon I've killed twenty of the little bastards, and they just keep coming,' screamed Bruce.

'Yeah, me too; how many of the pricks are there out there? Must be hundreds,' replied Ken.

'Feels like thousands.'

'You men follow me. They're trying to move around our flanks and we must stop them. We'll be dead if they succeed,' ordered Captain Templeton.

Ten men followed Captain Templeton to the rear of the airfield and encountered strong resistance. John was now the gunner, using a Lewis machine gun, as the original gunner had been fatally wounded. John strafed the enemy relentlessly, causing them to fall back, abandoning their flanking manoeuvre.

John on the Lewis Gun

Oivi 26 July

Templeton was trying to defend his position with about seventy-five Australian troops, all raw recruits, and a handful of local troops. Opposing him were several hundred battle hardened Japanese including the elite 5th Sasebo marines. The troops flown in from Port Moresby had not made it through yet and the Japanese were attacking aggressively, continually trying to encircle the Australian position.

Captain Templeton confided to his second in command, Sergeant Brian Wilcox, 'We can't withdraw, Brian. There's no way we can let these bastards take the Kokoda airfield. If they do, they'll be halfway to Moresby before they encounter C Company. It'll be a fucking bloodbath.'

'I agree, sir. I reckon we've got the balls to keep them busy here for as long as we need to. I hope the reinforcements they flew in arrive soon we could use a bit of help.'

Captain Templeton decided to sneak back behind the lines and head down the track towards Kokoda. His aim was to warn the second half of D Company that they were likely to encounter the enemy between them and where his troops were holding out.

As Templeton slipped down a steep embankment, a shot rang out. He died instantly.

The Japanese attack on the small Australian force was relentless, night was beginning to fall and the diggers faced annihilation. Major Watson of the Papuan Infantry Battalion had assumed command after Templeton failed to return. One of Watson's men, Lance Corporal Sanopa, saved the day. Once nightfall had descended, Sanopa led the troops to safely evacuate their position by a creek that flowed below Oivi. The track was teeming with Japanese, so that route was out of the question; the Papuan led them through thick jungle terrain until they reached the village of Denki just south of Kokoda.

Kokoda

Back at Kokoda, Lieutenant-Colonel Owen was waiting for news from Oivi. Owen knew they were having a tough time with few resources, as the second half of D Company sent to support them had to return to Kokoda as the track was controlled by the Japanese.

He did have some idea of the situation when a few soldiers who had escaped the encirclement of Oivi had reported that Templeton and his men were completely surrounded, and it seemed they were doomed.

Owen had only fifty men to defend Kokoda against a formable Japanese force. Knowing it was an impossible task, Owen decided to retreat to Denki. The troops carried as much as they could, and the remainder of the supplies were destroyed.

When his men reached Denki, Owen was delighted to find many of Templeton's men had survived thanks to Lance Corporal Sanopa.

Lance Corporal Sanopa

Owen now had a tough choice. He could either take his exhausted troops back along the track, or meet up with C Company, still four days away. With C Company and his one hundred and twenty men, Owen could create a stronghold as a defence against the Japanese. His other, more difficult, option was to return to Kokoda and hold it against the Japanese onslaught until reinforcements arrived from Port Moresby. He chose the latter option, knowing that the airstrip was the only feasible way to bring in men and supplies.

Owen was concerned that the one hundred and twenty men were exhausted, hungry, sick, and inadequately equipped, but Kokoda had to be saved.

Leaving twenty men behind at Deniki, Owen led one hundred young, inexperienced, inadequately dressed soldiers back to Kokoda. His intelligence indicated that five hundred crack Japanese troops were only a few hours from the Australian base.

The officer asked for a volunteer to stay back on the track and monitor the Japanese advance and return with news of their numbers and if they were carrying any heavy weapons. It was a dangerous assignment but vital to their successful defence of Kokoda.

Ken Jones volunteered, knowing the risks involved

Owen and his troops reached Kokoda by late morning and he deployed his men in defensive positions around the various buildings that made up the Australian administrative centre.

Once secured, he radioed Port Moresby, informed them of his intention to defend the airstrip and requested reinforcements and mortars.

Owen and his men waited, hoping the aircraft would arrive before the Japanese.

'Bloody hell, mate, I hope the birds get here soon. There's no way in hell we're going to be able to hold off the little pricks without more ammo,' said John.

'Don't worry, Owen's got it all sorted. I heard him on the radio to Moresby pleading his case,' replied Bruce.

'Can you hear that? It's a plane, I can hear a fucking plane— you bewdy.'

'There it is, shit, there are two of the buggers.'

Two American Douglas transport planes appeared over Kokoda and began circling the airstrip. They were carrying ammunition and reinforcements from the 39th Battalion. They could obviously see the Japanese moving towards the airstrip and were fearful they would arrive while they were unloading their precious cargo. The two pilots refused to land and returned to Port Moresby.

'They're heading back, the cowardly bastards! I don't fucking believe it,' yelled John.

'That's it, mate. We're well and truly fucked now!' exclaimed Bruce.

Owen was devastated, as was his small band of men. They were now well and truly on their own to face a powerful Japanese force.

The Australians all had their heads in their hands, knowing they were not long for this world. The bastards at HQ in their nice big offices sipping gin and tonic had abandoned them all.

THE GENTLE ART OF PERSUASION
CHAPTER 24

Ken camouflaged himself by using tree branches and rubbing dirt into his face. His khaki uniform didn't provide much camouflage, so the soldier stripped off his shirt and hid it under a rock.

Ken positioned himself about six feet off the track, hoping the Japs wouldn't discover him. Two hours later, about three hundred enemy soldiers had passed, and they just kept coming. It was starting to get dark, making his job even more difficult

Ken made the decision to move further into the jungle and rest for the night; his objective was to make it back to Kokoda next morning to report his findings. The digger was woken from his fitful sleep by the sensation of cold steel pushing against the back of his neck. A Japanese soldier was yelling at him, but Ken had no idea what he was saying. He soon got the picture, though; he was being ordered to his feet. The Jap pushed him in the back with his bayonet, forcing him back onto the track where a Japanese officer spoke to him in reasonable English.

'You are a spy, aren't you?'

'No, I lost my way trying to get back to my Battalion.'

'What Battalion?'

'The 42nd.'

'You are lying; I know you are with the 39th. How many of you at Kokoda?'

'I don't know, reinforcements have been flown in over the past few days. Maybe one thousand; maybe more.'

'I don't believe you. Only two planes have flown to Kokoda and they returned without landing, cowards. Take him away and tie him up. I'll interrogate him after I have eaten my dinner.'

Ken was tied by the wrists and ankles between two trees and left to contemplate his future for a couple of hours. The officer returned with two soldiers and began his questioning.

'I'll ask you once again; how many soldiers are defending Kokoda?'

'I don't know. Maybe two thousand.'

The officer nodded to the two privates; they both stuck their bayonets about an inch into Ken. Ken screamed.

'That might refresh your memory. I'll ask you again; how many troops defending Kokoda?'

'I don't know. Maybe two thousand.'

Again Ken received two bayonet wounds. The interrogation lasted two hours and by the time it finished, Ken had received over one hundred wounds but did not change his story despite being near death. Finally, the Japanese officer gave up. He withdrew his samurai sword from its scarab and swiftly decapitated the brave Australian. They left his body tied to the trees and inserted a stake into his head. They placed it on the track to welcome C Company when they passed through.

As the Australians pursued the retreating Japanese along the Kokoda Track, they came upon evidence that the Japanese had been eating captured Australian soldiers. After a fierce clash with the Japanese at Templeton's Crossing, an Australian patrol was forced to withdraw and leave behind six Australian dead and four wounded. Reinforcements arrived on the following day, and the Australians could attack again and capture the Japanese position. The Australians troops were horrified to find that the Japanese had been eating both the wounded and dead Australians who had been left behind on the previous day. Corporal Bill Hedges describes the ghastly scene:

> *The Japanese had cannibalised our wounded and dead soldiers. We found them with meat stripped off their legs and half-cooked meat in the Japanese dishes (pots)'.*

One of Corporal Hedge's closest comrades was among the butchered bodies.

> *'I was heartily disgusted and disappointed to see my good friend lying there, with the flesh stripped off his arms and legs; his uniform torn off him.'*

Shortly afterwards, the Australian corporal was appalled to discover that the Japanese had not resorted to cannibalism because of starvation.

> *'We found dumps with rice and a lot of tinned food. So they weren't starving and having to eat flesh because they were hungry.'*

July 28, 1942

Early in the evening of the 28th, the band of Australian soldiers at Kokoda could hear Japanese troops being deployed around their positions. Then, the firestorm erupted. The Japanese poured machine gun fire and mortars into the Kokoda defensive positions.

Lieutenant-Colonel Owen received a fatal wound to the head as the officer went from group to group reassuring and encouraging his men during the fight. Major Watson assumed command and although the Australians had only small arms, they put up a valiant fight. It could have been easier if Major General Morris had provided them with the mortars they had requested. According to Morris, they were not suitable to use in the conditions. The Japanese certainly proved their suitability.

By 2.30 a.m. on the 29th of July, and with a thick mist, drifting across the plateau the Japanese launched a full-scale assault. The Australians were expecting it and were determined to defend their airfield despite being abandoned by Morris in Port Moresby. The diggers fought desperately but were overwhelmed by the sheer numbers of Japanese coming at them.

Finally, Major Watson gave his troops the order to withdraw to Deniki. Firing as they retreated, and under cover of the thick mist, they disappeared into the rubber plantation bordering the field. The Japanese did not pursue them as they had achieved their objective. Kokoda was now in their hands.

The heroic stand against overwhelming odds by a much smaller force, the 39th Battalion militia troops (Chocos), with the help of the Papuan Infantry Battalion first at Oivi and then at Kokoda, demonstrates the Australian fighting spirit. The fact that the Australians were denied reinforcements and left on their own to fight the Japanese typifies the enormous struggles the Australian troops faced at Kokoda.

The same attitudes by the military hierarchy ensued with depressing regularity during the entire Kokoda campaign. It was always the case of too little too late.

The Australian troops and their field commanders would always find themselves hopelessly outnumbered; debilitated by almost constant rain and cold mountain nights; constantly denied adequate food, clothing, equipment, rest and reinforcements when they desperately needed them, and when they were fighting a fiercely determined enemy who was always better equipped and supplied than they were. To add to their sense of abandonment, they would also have to suffer deliberate minimisation of the difficulties they faced, deliberate understatement of Japanese numbers, and unjustified denigration of their fighting spirit by senior commanders in Australia who felt obliged to find scapegoats for their own neglect

It was only after the capture of Kokoda by the Japanese on the 29th of July, 1942, that MacArthur and Blamey appear to have appreciated the danger that Australia might face because of their neglect of the northern defences. Blamey ordered veteran troops of the AIF 7th Division to embark immediately for New Guinea. Troops of the 21st Brigade boarded a ship for Port Moresby on the 6th of August, 1942. Despite the determination and strength of the Japanese advance towards Kokoda, and even after its capture by them, General Blamey still believed that the Japanese were only intending to establish a forward base in the Gona-Buna area and were not intending to cross the Owen Stanley Range. Blamey held fast to his delusion that the Japanese did not intend to cross the Owen Stanley Range even when the Japanese had passed through Kokoda and had advanced down the Kokoda Track to Deniki. It is difficult to reach any conclusion other than that Blamey was inexcusably blinding himself to the clearest possible indication of Japan's intention to mount an overland attack on Port Moresby. If that conclusion is reached, it raises a real question concerning Blamey's fitness to command Australia's land forces at this time.

General Blamey

At the conclusion of the Kokoda campaign, the Japanese had been denied their quest to occupy Port Moresby.

The two Australian diggers from the 39th Battalion were sitting on the grass at Koitaki where the 39th had been sent to recuperate after the gruelling campaign.

John Healy and Bruce Cook had survived; sadly their good mate Ken Jones had not. After a month recuperating at Koitaki, the two soldiers went on to participate in the battle at Milne Bay and the capture of Lae.

They survived both these battles and were shipped home in 1944 on the same ship that had brought them to New Guinea; the *Duntroon*.

On the ship, the two friends discussed what they would do after the war and both decided they would apply for a farm under the Soldier Settlement Scheme.

I STILL CALL AUSTRALIA HOME
CHAPTER 25

January 1945
Puckapunyal Army Base Victoria

John and Bruce knew that they could be assigned anywhere, including taking part in the invasion of Japan with their brothers in arms from New Zealand Canada and Britain. The fact that they were now back in Australia meant little. They were not back with their families, but at Puckapunyal Army Base, learning new methods on how to kill the enemy more effectively.

Prior to the end of the war on the 15th of August, 1945, the Australian military was preparing to contribute forces to the invasion of Japan. Australia's participation in this operation would have involved elements of all three services fighting as part of Commonwealth forces. It was planned to form a new 10th Division from existing AIF personnel, which would form part of the Commonwealth with British, Canadian and New Zealand units. The corps' organisation was to be identical to a US Army corps, and it would have participated in the invasion of the Japanese home island of Honshū, which was scheduled for March 1946 under Operation Coronet. Planning for operations against Japan ceased in August 1945 when Japan surrendered following the atomic bombings of Hiroshima and Nagasaki.

Both soldiers were given three-day passes to travel to Melbourne and visit their families after they arrived back from Papua New Guinea. Their families weren't notified or told of their return due to security reasons so there was no fanfare at the dock when the *Duntroon* berthed at Prince's Pier. There was still a war going on and the Japanese didn't look like giving up anytime soon.

John knocked on the front door of 8 Henty Street Bentleigh. His mother, Margaret, answered the door. She just looked at John without uttering a sound and then she began to shake uncontrollably.

'Hello, Mum, aren't you going to give me a kiss? It's been a while since you've seen me.'

'John! It can't be! You're in New Guinea.'

'I got back a couple of weeks ago. Let me inside and I'll tell you all about it.'

Margaret flung open the flywire door and wrapped her arms around her son kissing him and crying at the same time. She wouldn't let him go. Ted came out to see what all the fuss was about. He saw his son and almost collapsed.

'John, I can't believe it! You're back.'

'G'day Dad, how are you, mate?'

'I'm good, very good now that you're home safely.'

The two men shook hands firmly, and then something happened that John had never seen before. His father hugged him and began crying. After things settled down, they all went into the kitchen, and Margaret made a cup of tea.

'If I'd known you were coming I would have baked some scones. I do have some Anzac biscuits I baked a couple of days ago. Will that do?'

'Mum, that'd be great, pretty appropriate I would have thought.'

'So John, when will you be discharged?'

'I don't know, Dad, there's still a war going on and judging by the training they're giving us I'd say I'm in for some more action.'

'I suppose they don't tell you much?'

'No mate, you know the drum.'

John enjoyed his leave, catching up with his sister that night. The remainder of his time was spent catching up with old friends and reacquainting himself with his old girlfriend, Sarah. She was very pleased to see him; John felt that he still might have a future with her, despite only writing to her twice in four years.

John and Bruce met up at Spencer Street Station for the trip back to base; Bruce had a very similar experience to John and found it difficult to say goodbye to his family.

The two diggers would never be redeployed; they remained at Puckapunyal until war's end and were discharged on the same day; November 11th, 1945 – Armistice Day. CC

Atomic Bomb Nagasaki Japan August 9 1945

APPRENTICE FARMERS
CHAPTER 26

John and Bruce talked about their ambitions to become farmers while they were stationed at Puckapunyal. They did have reservations about their ability to create a successful farm holding, as neither of them had any farming experience. John had been a brickies' labourer before the war, and Bruce had been a junior bank teller.

Both had submitted their applications to the Soldier Settlement Commission and were waiting on their notification to attend an interview.

It was John who received his letter from the commission first; Bruce received his two days later. Both were required to appear before the selection board on the same day, the 15th of January, 1946.

Suitably attired in borrowed suits, the two aspiring farmers arrived at the commission's offices together. John's interview was scheduled for 2pm while Bruce was allocated the 3pm time slot.

The Soldier Settlement Commission was housed in the Victorian Governments' Public Officers. The waiting room was very stark with little furniture and a few old magazines to read. John was called in and was instructed to sit at the board table while opposite him were three very distinguished elderly gentlemen who looked like members of the Melbourne Club.

Surprisingly, they began their questioning by asking about PNG and the Kokoda Track. John answered the committee member's questions to the best of his ability.

They seemed very impressed with his war record and then went on to ask him about his experience in farming. They were less impressed with the answers given in relation to rural management.

They asked for John to leave the room while the three members discussed his application. After about twenty minutes, the returned soldier was called back in.

'Corporal Healy, we are very impressed with you as a person; your war record, and the way you present yourself are exemplary. However, you have applied for a farm with the aid of low interest loans. This is Government money, and the commission must be confident that you have the skills and experience to make a success of it. We propose that you work on a farm for a period of two years. The commission will pay your wages for this period and locate a suitable farm for your apprenticeship as it were.'

'Well, I don't know what to say other than thank you for the opportunity.'

'Excellent, Corporal Healy, we'll be in touch with you soon.'

John left the boardroom with mixed emotions, on the one hand, he was disappointed but on the other, he was excited about getting the opportunity to learn the ropes before taking on his new career.

Bruce was made the same offer and gratefully accepted.

To their surprise, they were both assigned to the same property, *Glengordon*, just outside Shepparton in Victoria. The farm comprised over one thousand acres and ran eight hundred dairy cows; it was the biggest milk producer in the region.

John and Bruce travelled together on the train and the farm manager, Mr Doug Westgarth, met them at the station and drove them out to the property.

There were four houses on the farm including a magnificent homestead.

Glengordon Homestead

The apprentice farmers were shown their living quarters a few hundred yards from the main house. It certainly wasn't as elaborate as *Glengordon*, but it had three bedrooms, a slow combustion fire and a rudimentary kitchen with a gas stove. They were quite happy. Compared to the army quarters they had been putting up with at the base and the conditions they endured in New Guinea, it was pure luxury.

Their training began next day when they were required to wake at 4.30am and help herd the cows into the milking sheds.

The two former soldiers learned every aspect of dairy farming over the following two years, from milking cows to helping install vacuum milking machines to speed up the process.

They learned the correct temperature to store the milk and how to separate the cream.

They even assisted the local vet in delivering several calves.

All in all, it was a very well-rounded education, and at the end of their time at *Glengordon*, both John and Bruce felt comfortable about owning and running a dairy farm.

The owner of the dairy farm, Mr Ian Stewart, wrote a very strong letter of commendation to the Soldier Settlement Commission recommending them highly.

All that was to remain was receiving notification that the commission had accepted their application and notifying them where their land was located and the size of the property.

January 1949

John was sitting on his parents' front veranda reading the *Sun* newspaper. It was a typical summer day with the temperature hovering around ninety degrees Fahrenheit. In the distance, a man ran up the street waving a piece of paper. As he got closer, John could see it was his best mate, Bruce.

'What's all the fuss about, mate? You look as if you've won the lottery.'

'I reckon I have, mate; I've received my letter from the Board.'

'Yeah, what's it say?'

'I've been accepted as a soldier settler. They've given me a dairy farm in a place called *Yanakie*.

'Where the fuck is Yanakie or whatever it's called?'

'Apparently it's on Wilson's Promontory in Gippsland.'

'Geez, that sounds all right! How much land are they giving you?'

'Two hundred acres plus twenty Friesian cows.'

'Well mate, you'll be set; what about a house?'

'Yep, they will build a house as well. They've thought of everything.'

'You got the low-interest loan?'

'Sure did, and I don't have to make any payments for the first five years.'

'Well, mate, I hope I get my letter soon. I'm getting a bit edgy especially now that you've been approved.'

'Don't worry, if I got approved you'll be a shoo-in.'

Bruce was right; John had to wait only another day.

When his letter arrived, John couldn't believe it; his farm allocation was in the same area as Bruce's. The same conditions applied, including the Friesian cows and a house.

John couldn't wait to see his mate and ran up the street to Bruce's house. The two battle hardened soldiers began jigging around the lounge room. Finally, when things settled down, they looked at the estate map to determine where their farms were located. They were amazed; their farms backed on to one another; they would be neighbours.

March 1949

The Closer Land Commission managed the Soldier Settlement Scheme; it was this scheme that organised a truck to transport John and Bruce's worldly goods to Yanakie. The journey took a full day, departing Melbourne at 7am and arriving at the farms at 6pm.

The driver and the boys unloaded John's goods and chattels first and decided to bunk down in the farmhouse until next morning when they would travel to Bruce's farm and unload his possessions.

Once this task was completed, both men inspected their properties. It seemed to be ideal dairy country with rich green grass and plenty of water. Both the cottages had sea views from their verandas, all in all, it was a returned soldier's paradise.

As a part of the farm package both Bruce and John were allocated a Vanguard utility with a low-interest loan for getting around their properties. Until the utes were delivered they were restricted to the farm. The other delivery they were looking forward to was the Friesian cows, as without them they had no money-making assets.

It was two weeks of boredom and frustration before the cows finally arrived. The two friends helped each other unload the cattle and herd them into their front paddocks. Milking would begin the following day. The Vanguards arrived five days later and now they were fully operational.

1949 Vanguard

John and Bruce threw themselves into running their dairy farms and began reaping the benefits. They met regularly and apart from the social benefits, they learned from each other's farm management practices. Twelve months passed and although their herds were producing thirty-five thousand litres of milk a year it wasn't enough to make a living. The two dairy farmers decided to purchase another ten cows each with the aid of a low-interest loan from the commission. The following year they automated the milking process by installing the latest milking machines.

Over the following four years, they were able to increase their herds to seventy Friesians each. Both John and Bruce employed a full-time farm hand to help them work their properties and employed part-time workers to assist with the milking.

A significant change to their lives occurred when they both married local girls. It wasn't too long before they started families. John and Pam had a baby boy, and Bruce and Val had a girl.

One night when the two families were enjoying a barbecue, John suggested they should consider merging the two farms.

'Bruce, just think, if we merged, we would improve our buying power and we should be able to negotiate with the dairy for a better price for our milk.'

'Yeah, I see what you mean, mate. If we did, how would we structure it?'

'I reckon we incorporate, you know, form a company.'

'Bloody hell, mate, I don't know anything about companies and all that stuff.'

'You don't have to. We'll get the accountant to put it together for us.'

'What about the new houses we both just built? Who will own them?'

'I'm not sure, but the accountant will work that out.'

'Okay, let's arrange to see him as soon as.'

'I'll call him in the morning.'

'I suppose we'll have to come up with a name for the company.'

'Yeah, we'll come up with something.'

John rang Graham Patching the next morning and arranged an appointment for the following Wednesday. The two entrepreneurs explained their plan and asked Graham for his professional opinion. The accountant advised them they shouldn't rush into it on the basis that there were many things to consider, including the freehold for their houses.

Over the next three months and several meetings with Graham and their lawyer, Roger Baker, a decision was finally made; they would merge by creating a company. The name of this new enterprise would be *Kokoda*.

1 January 1956

Kokoda began trading as a proprietary limited company with joint managing directors and four shareholders.

The production of milk increased as the technology improved. By the time both John and Bruce retired in 1995, the yield per cow was:

Year ended 30 June	Litres
1960	1,959
1970	2,650
1980	2,848
1985	3,337
1990	3,781
1995	4,481

Kokoda, in 1995, boasted an annual milk production of 3,584,800 litres.

Simon Healy and Emma Cook took over from their parents as joint managing directors. The company continued to prosper.

John and Pam retired to the Gold Coast while Bruce and Val moved to Cowes, Phillip Island.

The two warriors who had survived the jungles of New Guinea and the ferocious Japanese enemy had turned adversity into a happy and prosperous life. They acknowledged the Closer Settlement farm scheme as the key to their success.

SUCCESS OR FAILURE?
CHAPTER 27

The Soldier Settlement Schemes implemented around Australia by the various State Governments were designed as a reward for returning soldiers who had put their lives on the line for their country. These schemes were implemented after both the first and second world wars.

They were also meant to solve the chronic unemployment situation after both wars.

There has been a misconception that farms were gifted to our soldiers; when in fact, they were sold, sometimes at inflated prices.

Loans below the then current interest rate were made available and in some cases foreclosed, forcing the soldiers off their land and back to the unemployment lines.

Criticism of the size of the farms and the quality of the land has been made, although the Government did seem to learn its lesson after the First World War. The farms were more sustainable after the Second World War.

Many of the soldiers who were allocated farms had no agricultural experience and despite some help, failed.

Farms that were carved out of large properties were often the land the owner didn't want and couldn't use.

Many farms had no access to roads or transport so that if they did have produce to sell they couldn't get it to market.

Loneliness was also a significant factor, causing many to take their own lives, often with the 303 they brought home from the war.

An example of success and failure can be seen in the table below.

The Subdivision of Estates for Soldier Settlement in the Western District – Victoria – Australia 1918-1930

Soldier Settler Estate	Year acquired.	Allotments Allocated	Allotment Forfeited	Allotments Re-disposed of	% of Allotments Forfeited
Chrome	1924	9	0	0	0
Ettrick	1919	3	0	0	0
Tahara	1920	6	0	0	0

Soldier Settler Estate	Year acquired.	Allotments Allocated	Allotment Forfeited	Allotments Re-disposed of	% of Allotments Forfeited
Hilgay	1920	34	0	0	0
Poligolet	1918	6	0	0	0
Nangeela	1920	15	0	0	0
Green Hills	1920	18	1	0	5
Koonongwootong N	1921	32	2	2	6
Narrapumelap	1921	52	5	2	10
Knebsworth	1923	19	2	1	11
Hensely Park	1921	14	2	2	14
Murndal	1919	7	1	1	14
Wooloongoon	1921	7	1	1	14
Glenorchy	1921	47	7	7	15
Mt Bute	1921	174	27	26	16
Warrong	1920	90	14	14	16
Shadwell Park	1920	25	4	4	16
Gringelona	1920	31	5	5	16
Gala	1919	5	1	1	20
Glenronald	1918	25	5	5	20
Chocolyn	1920	43	9	9	21
Struan	1919	61	13	10	21
Kolora	1921	42	9	9	21
Purrumbete S	1918	39	9	9	23
Terrinallum	1921	43	15	12	35
Derrinallum	1918	112	41	32	37
Koort Koort Nong	1921	30	11	9	37
Larra	1920	3	3	3	50
Korongah	1919	12	6	4	50
Mt Violet	1921	86	44	42	51
Wollaston	1919	19	10	10	53
Mt Elephant	1921	29	16	16	55

Soldier Settler Estate	Year acquired.	Allotments Allocated	Allotment Forfeited	Allotments Re-disposed of	% of Allotments Forfeited
Total		1141	260	237	23

Source: Collated from the reports of the Closer Settlement Board 1920-30, *Victorian Parliamentary Papers* 1920-30.

Mt Bute, Mt Violet, and Mt Elephant all stand out as high failure areas. These farms were on the granite belt of the Western Districts of Victoria.

In some areas, including Western Australia, the failure rate was over forty per cent.

Post World War One		
State	Farms Settled	Failure Rate
NSW	9302	29%
VIC	11,140	17%
QLD	6031	40%
SA	4082	33%
WA	5030	30%
TAS	1976	61%

Was the scheme a success or failure? Having read this book, I hope you will draw your own conclusions.

THE END

BIBLIOGRAPHY

www.wdm.ca/skteacherguide/WDMResearch/ImpactofWWI.pdf   http://www.wdm.ca/skteacherguide/WDMResearch/ImpactofWWI.pdf

olc.spsd.sk.ca/de/saskatchewan100/researchpapers/SAB papers/soildersettlement.pdf

1127-4697-1-PB.pdf

Before You Start an Apple Orchard - Commercial Fruit Production in Minnesota

Creating a Modern Countryside: Liberalism and Land Resettlement in British ... - James Murton - Google Books

Great Depression in Australia - Wikipedia, the free encyclopedia

Ancient Australian History

Thursday's Child: Great Depression

Enlistment statistics, First World War | Australian War Memorial

1127-4697-1-PB (2).pdf

Flinders Island - Tasmania - Islands of Australia

A Place of Their Own: The Men and Women of War Service Land Settlement at ... - Karen George - Google Books

Library Log in

011294136597345.pdf   file:///Users/garry/Downloads/011294136597345.pdf

The Kokoda Track | Australians in World War II | The Pacific War | The Australian Veterans' Accounts | Kokoda Veterans' Video Interviews

Kokoda: Overview

PAC-10001811_kokodawwII1_print.jpg (1179×3417)

Kokoda Trail Campaign | Australian War Memorial

Public Record Office Victoria online catalogue

Robinvale: an island of multiculturalism in Victoria - theage.com.au

Was World War 2 a continuation of World War 1? | Online Essays .com

HINGE LWR OVEN - Blanco - Cooking - Appliance Spare Parts - Northern Gas and Electric - Melbourne

Murder and cannibalism on the Kokoda Track

Battleground New Guinea and its Defenders

AN OVERVIEW OF THE KOKODA CAMPAIGN

Mundarra & Mundarra Park Soldier Settlement (WW2), Edenhope - Apsley, S-W Victoria, Australia

04 Nov 1920 - Soldier Settlement. PROGRESS IN WESTERN DISTRICT...

20 Sep 1920 - SOLDIER SETTLEMENT. Warrong Estate, Koroit.

The 5 Most Embarrassing Failures in the History of War | Cracked.com

Emu War - Wikipedia, the free encyclopedia

11th Battalion | Australian War Memorial

The Great Emu War: In which some large, flightless birds unwittingly foiled the Australian Army

1301.2 - Victorian Year Book (Soft cover), 1998

Dairy in Gippsland - GippsDairy

Yanakie Settlement – reunion and reminiscences - Foster Community Online

https://digitised-collections.unimelb.edu.au/bitstream/handle/11343/40360/312846_2007-0023-0397.pdf?sequence=1

Yanakie VIC 3960 - Google Maps

http://www.pacificwar.org.au/KokodaCampaign/KokodaOverview.html

ACKNOWLEDGMENTS

Sally Odgers Editor

Desma Pacitto Cover Designer

Preview Readers

G&F Threlfall

Guy Walton

First published 2020 by Crabtree Pty Ltd

Small Farm Warriors is a work of fiction. Any resemblance to real persons, living or dead, is purely coincidental.

ISBN: 978-0-6484869-4-7 (p/b)

ISBN: 978-0-6484869-5-4 (ebook)